Aren't we all *Lost* in this small world?

SURAJ BHARTI

Copyright Page

AREN'T WE ALL LOST IN THIS SMALL WORLD?

SURAJ BHARTI

Copyright © 2024 by Suraj Bharti

Suraj Bharti

bhartisuraj623@gmail.com

Publisher's Note:

This is a work of fiction. Names, characters, places, and incidents either are products of the author's imagination or are used fictitiously. Any resemblance to actual events, locales, or persons, living or dead, is entirely coincidental.

First Edition: December 2024

Cover Design by Shubham Bharti

ME AND MY CIGARETTE

Timeline: Year 2028

<u>Chapter 1</u>

Cigarette makes me sad. I've tried to quit many times, but when the craving hits… I *have* to give in. It feels like something takes control of me at that moment. And those couple of minutes take me on a journey, a brief journey back into my past… far back.

When I had a caring, understanding wife who never took me for granted. We planned for a child, a new home, and a future together. Life was going smoothly, almost perfectly, and both sides of our families were happy, too, given that it was an arranged marriage.

But then, everything *woofed…* in an instant.

On October 8, 2024, she died in a car accident. It was instant—a spot death. I didn't even get the chance to see her on her last breath.

It's been almost four years, but I still think of her…especially when I smoke. I think that's why I can't quit since smoking is my only way to trigger back those memories. But once the cigarette burns out, all I'm left with is a regret, that I'm going nowhere but towards *more* darkness.

When I first started smoking, I cried a lot, always thinking of her. My friends said it was good, that I was finally releasing my grief. But I don't think it's a release. I've been smoking for two years now, and I still feel the same about her. I still cry…just silently now.

Her name was Rangoli, but to me, she was my Rung, the one who brought so much color into my life. I never imagined I'd end up with a girl like her—so beautiful and full of life. All the credit goes to my mom, my wing-woman, who first saw her at a wedding. My mom went straight to her parents and showed them my picture. The next day, I found out they wanted to meet me.

We went to her house, and I was waiting to see her for the first time while her parents and my parents were chatting on the couch. I was nervous because I never trusted my mom's choices.

But not this time. She came into the living room with tea for us. She didn't even meet my eyes, pretending to be shy, likely because her parents told her to. But I couldn't stop looking at her. She was nervous too.

She sat down with us, and soon her mom started bragging about her cooking skills, while my mom pretended to appreciate everything. After some time, our parents suggested that Rung and I talk privately.

When we got to her bedroom, I noticed posters of athletes I didn't recognize.

"Wow, do you like sports?" I asked.

"Yes, I play badminton for states," she replied.

"Wow! That's impressive," I said.

But her face grew sad. "But what's the point? I'll have to give it up when I get married."

I smiled at her and said, "I promise, if everything works out and we get married, you won't have to give up your game."

"Really?" she said, her face lighting up.

"Yeah. I've always wanted to marry someone passionate about something. I don't need a housewife waiting for me to come home at night. And also, I'm a chef, so I don't need anyone to cook for me."

She looked straight into my eyes and smirked. "Wow, are you for real?" she said, then playfully tickled my hand.

"Ouch!" I responded. Then I added, "Haha, I know I say big things sometimes, but I have my flaws too."

"Well, who doesn't have flaws? We're all human, right?" she replied.

"True." I nod.

She thought for a moment before asking, "By the way, what are your flaws?"

I paused, then smiled. "My anger. It can be... dangerous."

"Don't worry, we'll work on that," she said. Then she realized it was too soon, so she quickly added, "Oh, sorry."

I blushed and said softly, "It's okay," trying to comfort her.

It felt like the perfect arranged marriage date for both of us.

Her gaze dropped slightly, and she hesitated before saying, "I have my flaws too."

"Oh yeah? What's that?" I asked instantly.

"I'm terrible at cooking. Actually, my mom made the lunch today, not me," she admitted.

I laughed. "Oh!"

"Yeah."

I looked at her with a grin. "Don't worry, we'll work on that."

We both laughed.

We were a perfect match from day one. And, we never fought in those two years. She was all I needed in my life, and we both became codependent on each other, that the day she died, I was unable to show emotions to people. I was not responding. And I was so mad at her that she didn't keep her promises.

I was lost.

And I think I still am… after four years.

Chapter 2

"Pass me the chocolate syrup," Monty says.

(Monty is my colleague chef).

I pass Monty the syrup, and looking at him who has been preparing the cake for almost half an hour in the hotel's kitchen, I ask, "Hey, what's the occasion?"

He replies, "It's the birthday of the hotel's owner. And they want this cake to be special."

"Oh, what's his name?" I inquire.

"Rishi Barman," he says casually. "Don't you know that?"

"No, I didn't."

But I'm trying to remember because I've heard this name before. So, I say, confused, "Rishi Barman? I've heard this name before, but not from here. I can't remember."

Monty clarifies, "Yeah, Rishi's also a famous writer. I've read his books."

"Yes! Now, I'm remember. I've one of his books in my house," I say a little loud.

"Really?" he smirks. "Since when did you start reading books? I thought you were just a movie person."

"No, it belonged to Rung, my wife. She was really into romance novels back then," I reply.

Monty pauses, thinking, then says, "Oh! You must be confused because Rishi only writes non-fiction books."

"Really?" I shrug. But then I say out of boredom, "Okay, whatever man. Why do we care so much about what this guy writes? Is your cake ready now? Let's go out for a smoke."

He smiles. "Yeah, I'm done. Let's go."

###

I'm home, going through Rung's old stuff in our storeroom. I'm looking for that book by Rishi Barman because I'm sure it's not non-fiction. But everything is so messed up here with spiderwebs and dust. There are so many books sitting one upon another. To be honest, I'm not quite interested in books, but because Rung had this book, and most probably she had read it, so I think maybe I'll give it a try if it's good. Maybe just a few pages.

And I'm pretty sure it's a romance novel.

I finally found it, light blue cover as I remember. Wiping the dust off the book cover, I can now clearly see the book's title. It's called, "Pieces of You… A romance novel by Rishi Barman."

It doesn't look like a non-fiction now. I smirk.

'Well, let's check out the book reviews on the internet,' I think.

I have this thing these days, I go for reviews before trying anything new, whether it's some movie or a new restaurant. It's not that I blindly trust people's opinions, the actual reason is that I'm at a stage in life where I get bored easily. So, if I'm trying anything new, I must be sure that it's at least decent. And I since haven't read any book my college, so if *this* book is shitty, I probably regret it.

I google it. 'Pieces of You by Rishi Barman reviews.'

But I don't find any website that reviews this book on Google's top search results. Just some spam websites pop up.

Not a single review? It's like this book never existed. That's odd.

I'm scrolling through the search page to get anything about this book.

I find a Reddit post. It's from four years ago, as I read…

"26th June, 2024

Chetan69

Hi, I'm Chetan, and best friend of Rishi Barman (the upcoming star in the literary field). I'm drunk right now, and I'm with Rishi and one more friend. They are sleeping. It's 2 am now. If you're reading this post, then you might have searched for this book, "Pieces of You" by Rishi. But unfortunately, he has unpublished this book today from every platform, because of his 'so-called girlfriend'. I cannot say her name here, and guys honestly, she doesn't deserve it. She left him and moved to Canada five months ago, but our Rishi still loves her like crazy.

Actually, Rishi wrote this book to show his love for her, and it was about their true love story. And when she read this book, she told him that he should have asked her before writing this story. She said it contains details about them, and she's concerned about her reputation. I don't know why she said that.

In his defense, he told her that the character names and the scene settings are different, because of their privacy. So, what was the problem? Only she knows.

After their fight, he had to unpublish the book just five days after publishing it. Rishi said to me, "I'm fine if the book is unpublished. I guess now this book was only meant for her, not for the world. But I'm glad that she read it."

Such a lover…or a loser in love? You decide, guys.

I'm exhausted… and I'm drunk. But I'm happy in the sense that I'm with my friends after so long.

So, if you have this book, you guys are very lucky and Rishi's truest fans because he told me only 8 copies were sold before unpublishing. And as being his best friend, I would say to you all, don't give up on this guy. He has been through a lot. But he's a passionate writer. He will come back strong.

I think he's the chosen one guys…

Okay, bye, guys. Good night."

.

.

I sensed there was something fishy when I didn't see any reviews for the book.

But, that's sad!

I'm glad Rishi did big in his future. Technically, he's my boss now. I think I should meet and congratulate him one day.

And now I know Rung was his big fan because only 8 copies were sold before unpublishing this book and she had one of them. That's crazy! … and honestly, I think now I'm ready to read this book.

But then I accidentally scroll down to this Reddit post.

"Wait, What!!!"

No way!

Rung replied to this Reddit post when she was alive.

I'm reading…

'Rangoli06738

3ʳᵈ October, 2024

I'm Rangoli and I've read this book. I think it's a shame that Rishi had to unpublish this beautiful book. It took me just 3 hours to read the whole book because it was a page-turner for me. And I found myself crying after the book ended. I'm sure his girlfriend didn't even read the whole book…

I hope Rishi finds some peace because writing a book isn't a piece of cake, and unpublishing it? I can't imagine what he went through.

I just loved the book, and I felt so much throughout. I wish I could review this book, but this book doesn't exist anymore. I feel sad. Anyway, five stars from my side.

And, and, and… If we're writing about love without asking our lovers, sorry Rishi! Hehe. I also want to share something with the whole world without asking my beautiful lover.

I also love someone, and I'm blushing right now…He is my husband, but also my best friend. Every time I see him, I fall in love with him. It's been 2 years since our marriage, but we never fought. It's crazy… We used to be two different people, but now I think we both are the same. I play badminton for India, and he's a professional chef. But he wakes up early just to practice badminton with me. And when he comes home from work, I cook for him. Well, I try. He's my soulmate that I didn't have to find. His mother found me. Big shoutout to her…my lady. Arrange marriage rocks!

And now someone special is coming to our house. I'm 2 months pregnant.

I don't know if you'll ever read this my dear husband, but this is for you, "First, I'm sorry for writing this. If something happens to me, I know you won't like me saying this. I don't know why I'm saying this right now, maybe I'm emotional after reading this book. But let's say for a 1 percent chance that if something happens to me in the future, please don't forget to move on my love. I know I am not very good at giving speeches, but I don't like when you keep saying that we're codependent, and you cannot live without me. And you say this, feeling proud. I never told you but it haunts me when you say that. I worry sometimes about how you will live after me.

We are not codependent, my love! We are perfect, even without each other. You complete yourself. And that's why I love you Kanan. You were already perfect when you came to my house for the first time, that's why I chose you. And I never stopped trusting you, because you're still perfect. And you will be always…even without me. I'm sorry for writing this.

But I know there's not a chance you can read this.

Love you, my personal chef!" Forever Yours' Rung."

.

.

.

My tears fall as I think, 'I'm…I am so angry at you right now, Rung. What if I was dead instead of you? Would it be easy for you to move on? I don't think so. I know you were as codependent as I was. Writing something is very easy, Rung. And how did you know something would happen to you? Because you wrote this just five days before your… Now, I think I didn't know you well enough.'

I light up a cigarette.

Chapter 3

I couldn't sleep last night and don't feel like going to work today. I was up all night thinking about Rung, smoking way too many cigarettes and finally ended up reading the book.

I think the book was just Okay, definitely not a five-star though.

Whatever it is, I want to stay home today, and I'll try not to smoke. I'll order something nice and watch a movie online because I don't feel like getting out of bed.

I'm in my thoughts, lying under the blanket, when my phone starts ringing.

It's Monty.

Picking up, he yells, "Where are you? It's 12."

I reply, "Monty, I can't come to work. Please manage for today."

"Okay, but what happened? You never take leaves," he asks softly but confusedly.

"Just…please understand man. I want to be alone," I reply.

"Okay, don't worry, I'll manage here," he replies.

I'm watching a movie when the doorbell rings. Getting up to answer it, but when I glance out the window, I see Monty standing outside and it makes me mad.

As I open the door, I lecture, "What part of 'I wanted to be alone today' don't you understand?"

He smiles while replying, "Man, I was just worried about you, because you never take leaves. I thought you needed a company to talk to."

I shake my head, clearly not impressed. "Fine, come in."

I notice a book in his hand. Sitting on the couch, he puts a book on the coffee table. I point to the book, feeling confused.

"Oh, this? It's for you," he says, handing me the book.

"What's it about?" I ask, but my attention shifts to the author's name: Rishi Barman.

"I think you should read it," he says. "It's called *Let's Heal Together*, written by our writer friend. It came out last year and became a number-one bestseller in the non-fiction category. I have a feeling you'll like it."

"No, I don't like his books," I reply without hesitation, placing the book on the coffee table.

"But how can you say that? You haven't read his books," he says.

"Actually, I did. I read one of his books yesterday. It was just full of love and stuff. No climax, no drama," I explain.

"Oh, so it's a romance book?" he asks.

"Yeah," I respond.

He looks at me and starts laughing.

"What's so funny?" I ask, frowning.

He chuckles. "Why on earth did you think you'd enjoy a romance book with everything you're going through? Romance is the last thing you need right now." Pointing to the book he brought, he adds, "You need this one. I've heard it's helped a lot of people."

I narrow my eyes at him and ask, "Do you think I'm so messed up that I need a self-help book?"

He fumbles, "No... no, that's not what I'm saying. But I do think this book might have something for you. Trust me, you'll have to read it to find out."

I keep staring at him, wondering why he's so insistent about this book—especially since he never lends me books.

He quickly adds, "Okay, fine. I'll just leave it here. Now I've got to go. See you soon, my friend… probably in the kitchen."

I shake my head as he stands up. I walk him to the main door and watch as he leaves.

###

I binge-watched three movies after Monty left and it was quite a good day. So, I walk into the living room to smoke. It's 9 pm.

As I strike a match, a cool breeze flows in through the window and blows it out. I can't light my cigarette. But the wind does manage to open the book on the coffee table, and it lands somewhere in the middle.

I can clearly see a passage on the page, titled *'ME AND MY CIGARETTE'* in the book.

It catches my attention.

Is it just a coincidence that I was about to light a cigarette and the page happens to be about one?

Then I notice the page has been folded at the top. That's why it opened up when the wind hit it.

So, not a total coincidence. Monty must have wanted me to read this specific passage, which is why he folded the page.

But I'm in confusion right now. Should I light up my cigarette or not? The topic is tempting.

Aah! What the hell? I light up my cigarette and start reading…

"Me and my cigarette

I look at your picture while smoking a cigarette. Even after years, you're gone now, I can feel you fresh, just as you left; Your lavender smell. I don't know if I can ever forget you. I don't know if you still read my words, but if you do…you will find 'pieces of you' everywhere, scattered in my world. I don't know how many lovers out there like me talk to their cigarettes. I wish their souls get fixed.

I don't crave cigarettes, actually this I get to know now after a couple of years. I think I crave for the moment cigarette helps me to get there. And I want to live in those moments, but I'm also aware that they both aren't good for my health now: the cigarettes and **the moments** *I spent with you. I want to quit and also don't want to. It's dicey and I'm afraid that if I stopped smoking, I may forget you and…those blurry moments that I'm still carrying with me.*

But I think it's time. It's time to say goodbye to this little friend. I know it will be hard, but isn't every goodbye hard? Slowly slowly, every day, everything will fade away. You, the moments, and the cigarettes.

Healing is not running away. It's accepting things."

.

.

I exhale deeply.

"He's still in love with her."

Why is this guy so emotional and so deep? He is delusional, I think.

Why won't he just go to Canada to live with her for the rest of his life? I will ask him someday if he comes to the hotel.

God, why do people complicate love so much? I sigh.

I miss you, Rung, and I wish you were alive.

There's more written in the passage, but I think I get what he wants to say.

Chapter 4

It's a great day today, I don't know but I feel so light. After so long, I'm in a good mood today, maybe it was the book I read last night. I like this guy, Rishi. No wonder why Rung was his fan. This guy is so on point sometimes.

My phone rings. It's Monty, again.

I pick up the call.

"Bro, the hotel manager is not happy with you. He said you're not even picking up his call now?" Monty says.

"Forget that, I think I need a little break from everything," I reply.

"What do you mean, everything?"

I hesitate, "I don't know. I just want to take a small break… Maybe we can go to Goa? What say?"

Monty enthusiastically responds, "Yeah, I've been telling you that for a long time. But what happened to you suddenly?" He chuckles.

I pause for a moment. I say, "I read the book you gave me."

Monty laughs. "Oh! Did you like it? And congratulations on finally being his fan."

"Yeah man, I think I should thank him."

"Yeah, you can. He's our boss, remember," he replies.

"Yeah, I know."

"So, what are you gonna do today? Watch more movies?" he asks sarcastically.

I'm staring at a big picture of my beloved wife, Rung, playing badminton on the living room wall.

"Bro, can we go play badminton today?" I ask.

"No, I can't. Since you aren't coming to the kitchen, I have to handle everything here," he replies.

"Sorry Monty, I can't come for a few more days," I apologize.

"Don't worry, I'll handle everything here." He continues after thinking for a second, "Wait, we can go play cricket today. Nearby there's a playground for kids. We can play with them, just like the old times. I can take half an hour break,"

"Yeah, that's a great idea," I respond enthusiastically. "Thanks, bro… For everything."

He's been silent, but then he responds, "Gay!" He giggles. "Your name should be Kanan… Gay. Look, it also rhymes with Ray."

I laugh.

As he continues, "You don't have to thank me… ever. You're my brother."

"Thanks, man."

THE NEVER-ENDING NIGHT

Timeline: Year 2024

Chapter 1

After drinking four tequila shots and sitting on a pub bar stool for almost half an hour, I look at the bartender and finally speak in boredom, "Man, this place is dead! I mean where are the girls?"

The bartender looks annoyed at me and responds, "It's Thursday. What do you expect?"

I interrupt, "Yeah, but not a single girl in a bar?"

The bartender wipes down the counter. "Just wait for the DJ," he replies, his tone bitter. With a slight nod, he mutters, "I don't know where these guys keep coming from."

I can't say I like his tone, but I'm drunk, so I let it go. Instead, I say loudly, "Fine. I'm not going anywhere. I'll wait."

Too drunk to care, I lean over the bar and rest my head on the counter.

Then, after a while, I hear a voice. "Two glasses of whiskey, please," A girl says walking up to the bar.

My eyes open, and suddenly, the place is *buzzing*. Girls are everywhere!

"Wow," I whisper in awe.

The bartender leans in and whispers in my ear, "Still boring, huh?"

I grin. "Sorry, I take it back, friend," I reply. "How long was I out?"

He pauses for a moment before answering, "About an hour."

"An hour?" I exclaim. "Why didn't you wake me up?"

He looks at me, unfazed. "Because I'm busy." Then, with a wave of his hand, he adds, "Now, leave me alone, I have other customers."

"That's rude," I say, leaving my new bartender friend behind, and stepping into the next room. The place is packed, bodies swaying to the DJ's beats.

I smile. "Now this is my kind of scene."

"Hi! I'm **Chetan**, good-looking, confident... and if anyone wants to call me a Casanova, playboy, or even a fuckboy, yeah, go ahead, I am actually these things. But don't call me a pervert, I hate this word.

How can I describe this? Umm, I just love girls... and I respect them. Just not the commitment. Yeah, that's not my thing, sorry. Call it trust issues or whatever—I just like to keep my life simple.

Speaking more about myself—well, aside from my good looks, I have another superpower, my dancing. It's my secret weapon. So, I come to these pubs to show off my greatest talent—dancing… for all the single girls. And guess what? It works all the time… most of the time.

I wasn't always like this. Well, I was always awesome, like fucking awesome, but back then I had a wingman: my best friend, Rishi. We were partners in crime. God, I miss those days, when he helped me get dates.

He's a smart guy, but never used it for his benefit. I never understood why.

Then, something happened that always weakens a good friendship. Rishi met a girl at our college in Delhi.

Saloni.

Rishi and Saloni were just friends for four years in college, but after college, they moved in without telling anyone. And now after 7-8 years they are still together living in Delhi.

It's like Rishi's stuck in a cave, for those 7-8 years. A pussy cave. And he can't see what's going on outside of it.

Well, even though I don't know what's happening in his life right now, he barely calls me.

But I know one day he'll realize that good friends are everything.

So, last year in 2023, I got a good job offer in Bombay… I left Delhi—I left Rishi behind, and moved to Bombay."

On the dance floor of the pub now, I'm showing off my best moves to some random people, who are dancing along with the beat. And I've been observing a girl for almost 10 minutes now, dancing just in front of me and she's alone.

So, I tap her shoulder. The music is loud. "Hey," I shout.

Slowly turning around and facing me, she replies, "Sorry, I have a boyfriend," with an attitude, and she turns back around.

"Oh, okay." I nod.

That was the smallest talk ever!

Well, I didn't get rejected. She had a boyfriend. It's just the beginning and I'm still confident.

Look! We must not stop. That's the key while picking up girls.

But yeah, if you can read a girl's face, not her mind though, because no one can read a girl's mind.

So, if you can read a girl's face, you can be unstoppable. Like for real! It's an art.

I move myself to the corner of the room and glance around, my eyes sharp, scanning for girls as the flickering lights pulse in sync with the DJ's beats.

Within 2 minutes, I spot a girl sitting alone at the bar counter with short hair, thin arms, and big eyes, she's sipping her drink.

How could I possibly miss this? She's cute.

I walk over, lean in a bit, and say, "Hey, can I get you a drink?"

Her eyes meet mine.

"Sure, you can," she says with a drunken tone, her eyes tiny as she smiles. "But I know you just want to sleep with me."

What? She didn't even hesitate saying that.

What happened to all the girls here? Why am I getting such responses tonight? Am I too obvious, looking like a bad guy?' I'm thinking.

Her words throw me off, and I freeze, not sure how to respond. I mean, yeah, I do want to…sleep with her, but I like a little build-up, a little romance before that.

"Don't be shy," she smirks. "I know exactly what's on your mind."

What!

My eyes stuck, unsure how to react. So, I smile looking at her… but I think it was weird.

Can she actually read my mind?

I haven't said a word since I offered her the drink… Just my expressions. *Maybe I should say something now.*

But she beats me again to it. "Look, if all you want is sex, I'm game. But if you're looking for something serious… you are looking at the wrong place my friend," she says with a serious tone.

Ohhh!

Now, I feel slightly relaxed.

She's not any mind reader,

She's just like me. No strings attached.

But I'm still smiling weirdly.

Wait, why am I still talking to myself?

She turns away after not getting any verbal response from my side. Her attention shifts back to the bar, but I can feel a change in her energy.

Her expression changes completely, and for the first time, she looks… sad now. I can see her tears that she's trying to hide.

I step closer, trying to soften the mood. I finally say, "Hey, are you okay? We don't have to rush into anything. We can just talk if you're sad." I place my hand gently on hers and smile.

But she pulls her hand away and buries her face in her arms on the bar. I stand there, confused.

Did I say something wrong? I think.

"Leave me alone," she mutters, her head still down.

The bartender glances over, but the music is too loud to catch what's happening.

I don't get it. She came on strong, and now she's pushing me away.

What a psycho!

Feeling frustrated, I walk outside to smoke a cigarette.

###

20 minutes later, I'm standing outside the pub feeling the cool breeze.

I see her walking out of the pub, heading straight for me. She's smiling now and stops in front of me. "Can we start over?" she says.

I look at her, and I'm thinking, *'Really? After that?'*

But instead, I say, "Yeah, sure."

She looks a little embarrassed but still keeps her smile. "I'm sorry, man. My head's all over the place right now. You were being so nice, and… I'm not usually like that. The whole talk just came out in the moment. Don't judge me, I'm not that kind of girl."

"Oh, okay?" I raise an eyebrow, intrigued.

She nods. "Yeah."

I break the silence and ask, "So, go on. I want to know more about…what kind of girl you are then?"

"What kind?" She laughs softly. "I'm a good girl," she says and stops.

My eyes narrow. "Good girl! … Just a good girl? What does that even mean?" I say laughing as I expect to hear more from her.

She smiles awkwardly. "Don't laugh. I've been through enough," she says, then stops again, putting her face down like she doesn't really want to share.

I study her face for a few seconds and ask, "Why do you always stop when I'm actually listening?"

Giving me a sharp look, she replies instantly, "Because you're a stranger. I don't trust you."

"Then don't trust me. What are you doing here, talking with me?" I say, raising my voice a little.

She passes a sad look. "Okay, then," she says.

She's going back inside the bar, and I don't stop her.

But after going back for a few steps, she turns again and steps up to me.

'Ugh! Are you kidding me?' I think.

Now finally she blurts out, "Well I used to be the happy kind of girl." She coughs before continuing, "But three months ago, I had a rough breakup with a guy I dated for two years, who was continuously cheating on me. And the thing is I knew it. But still, I stuck around, thinking he'd change someday… But he didn't." She stops and sighs.

"Oh, that's sad," I whisper, and trying to comfort her.

She shouts, "All men are the same… Pigs."

I look around, and people are staring at us.

"Pigs? Excuse me?" I say, hesitating.

She sighs, then laughs apologetically. "Sorry, sorry… I don't know why I said that. Not you. You seem like a… decent guy."

She's depressed. I can tell from her behavior changes. And also, I can feel that she's still drunk.

"Yeah, I'm a decent guy," I reply. "Maybe I can't commit to anyone, but that doesn't make me a…pig," I say.

"No, no, of course not. But you're honest from the start, right?" she supports with a nod.

'Of course, I'm honest,' I think.

I reply, "Exactly! … I tell every girl that 'don't expect anything from me.'"

Slightly narrowing her eyes, she says, "Wait, what?" She chuckles but acts confused for a few seconds. "Every girl? How many girls are we talking about here?" she asks curiously.

"Thirty-two," I reply.

She takes a step backward. "Thirty-two?" she exclaims. "You've been with thirty-two girls? Who are you… a Greek god?" She laughs.

I blush and whisper, "Yeah, you can say that."

With a smirk, she replies, "Well, there's nothing to be proud of… You know it's not healthy right?"

"Oh, come on," I protest.

She nods. "Okay, fine."

A brief silence falls between us.

I break the silence. "So, what happened after that? You're moved on, now?" I ask.

"Oh, yeah." She pauses, thinking, then continues, "After the breakup, I locked myself in my house for three months, so that no one can contact me, not even my friends."

"Oh, really? You were in a house arrest?" I ask.

"Yeah, you can say that," she nods. "And you know tonight… this is my first time out after those three months," she says smiling, widening her eyes.

"Oh, really!" I gasp.

Oh, now I understand why she's behaving so weirdly: She forgot how to actually communicate with humans in those three months.

I ask smiling, "So, how's it feel finally being back out in the real world?"

She glances down, her smile fading slightly. "I guess it feels good now. But I was feeling sad when I came here, so I downed two vodka shots."

"Oh, that's fair," I say to support her. "After three months, you definitely earned those vodkas."

She looks up at me with emotional eyes and chuckles. "You're funny."

And another beat of silence lingers between us.

Sensing my hesitation, she asks, "What?"

"Nothing," I reply.

"No, what?" she insists, tapping my hand.

I whisper, "You know, calling someone funny often leads to…"

"Leads to what?" she asks with a confused smile. She repeats, "Leads to what?" Then she guesses, "Sex?"

I laugh covering my mouth. "I didn't say that."

"Oh, come on. I was only complimenting you that you're funny. Why's that come to your mind?" she teases.

"What? But you started it, inside the bar. I thought maybe you're still interested."

"Yeah, but I told you I don't know where it all came from. Maybe the vodka?" she says with a carefree smile.

This is getting me a little down. I've been rejected by two girls till now. I think I'll go home alone tonight.

She grins. "Okay, okay. Now, it's your turn to tell the story. Tell me why are you like this?"

"Oh, why am I this awesome?" I ask.

"Not awesome, but yeah, whatever. Continue," she interrupts.

"Honestly, I don't know. I don't have any story about being left or cheated on, that turned me into this… I like girls and want to keep things simple." I pause to think, then add, "You know I've watched my friend Rishi go through heartbreaks with the same girl over and over, and it hurts to see him like that… I just don't wanna be like him."

She nods. "Okay, so maybe that's your problem," she replies. "It made you stop trusting girls."

I protest, "First, stop labeling it as a problem. I don't think it's a problem for me."

"No, no, that's not what I'm saying," she defends. "But at some point, you're going to commit to someone, right?"

"Why? What's wrong with this? And why are you giving me this lecture right now?" I ask a little annoyed.

"I'm not lecturing you," she replies, her tone a little loud. "Look at me… I broke up, but that doesn't mean I will stop trusting guys."

I shake my head in disapproval.

She's really pissing me off right now.

"Okay, you told me about your friend's story. How about I tell you about my friend now?" she insists.

"Okay. Go on," I reply, but I'm interested.

"Okay, so she's a very good person, like a really good one. But once she wanted to explore… you know for a bit." She smiles hesitantly and continues, "So, she tried a dating app."

"Oh, now we're talking!" I smile.

She continues ignoring me, "And she had a few meaningless flings through it. She was enjoying her new life, just like you are now… But… but, listen carefully… slowly time passed and she didn't understand that when she got trapped in that loop. Every time she was with someone, she started to feel more empty. Her life became miserable and she got *addicted*… Addicted to… you know." She takes a heavy breath. "Finally, she had to take mental health counseling… and thank god finally she recovered, she's fine now."

I don't know how to respond to this because she just isn't getting it. She's just imposing her opinion on me.

I ask in a low tone, "So, what do you suggest then?"

She looks into my eyes and says softly, "I'm just saying, find a girl and fall in love with her, just once, and then choose your lifestyle."

I laugh softly, my voice low. "Where do I find this girl? Are girls even loyal these days?"

She narrows her eyes. "Yeah, many girls are loyal that I know." She smirks. "The real question is, 'Are you loyal?'" she counters.

Am I loyal? That's a really good question.

I reply, "Maybe. I've never had a relationship."

She smirks and looks away.

What does she want exactly?

Does she want me to ask her out?

She's too difficult to understand.

"Okay, wait here. I'm coming back," she says heading inside the pub.

"Where?" I ask, waving my hand.

She stops, saying, "To pee. Would you like to join me?"

"No, no." I laugh. She goes inside the pub.

.

.

.

10 minutes later, she again comes outside.

And I think I'm ready now.

She asks casually, "So? What are your thoughts?"

But I counter immediately, "Do you like me?" smiling staring at her face.

Her gaze shifts towards me, our eyes stuck for a couple of seconds before she smiles and answers, "Why do you think so?"

I reply without blinking, "I don't know. You tell me."

She says, "No, I don't like you. But I'll be happy if you change your path. It's not right for…"

I interrupt quickly, "Just like you changed your path?"

"Excuse me?" she says confused.

I shout, my eyes narrowed, "Oh, cut the crap now."

"What are you talking about?" she asks.

"Really?" I stare into her eyes. "Okay, so why did you ask me for sex inside the pub?"

"Why are you asking it again? I told you I was drunk, so I have no idea how it came out," she replies.

"So, when you're drunk, you become just like your friend from the story you told me?" I pause to check her reaction. And suddenly her gaze is downwards, confused, and her behavior changes. Then, I ask, "Or was it your story?"

And her gaze suddenly comes back to me, her eyes broad and stunned.

I grin. "Man! I knew it was your own story," I shout in excitement.

And it made her uncomfortable. "I have to go now. I'm getting late," she replies like she's in a hurry.

"No, wait," I say holding her hand. "I don't wanna make fun of you. And I know you don't like me. You only want to change me, but you know… I'm happy with what I am right now. Maybe I'll change my path one day like you did. But I don't feel, you know…like I'm shallow right now. I think my life's *awesome.*"

She nods slowly, but she doesn't say anything.

After a few seconds, I add, "Would you like to say something to that?"

"Yeah, maybe you don't need to change, you're glowing right now… I only tried to change you so you don't have to suffer like I did."

"Not a problem at all. You did what you felt right," I say, smiling. "But I'm also glad you're in a happy place right now."

She nods. "Thank you," she whispers and adds with a curious tone, "But I have one last question: How did you find out about it? Only my close friends know about my secret."

I giggle while saying, "You gave me 10 minutes to think when you were in the bathroom. That was your biggest mistake."

"What? Sorry, but what does that mean?" she asks, confused.

"It means I'm an overthinker… just like a few of my friends. It's a coincidence." I chuckle and continue, "And you can't give

enough time to the overthinkers and expect that your lies are safe…
We literally maintain a journal so that we empty our messed up heads
every night."

"Who all?" she asks.

"My friends, and me, we are overthinkers. Are you even
listening?" I reply.

"Okay, enough praising your friends. Can you only explain how
you figured it out?" she says, sounding irritated but still curious.

"Sorry, I just miss my friends sometimes…" I chuckle, my eyes
widen. "But, whatever… So, coming back to your story… I
think…you only sounded genuine while we were inside the bar when
we had *the interesting chat* of the whole night… and when you were
telling your 'friend's' story. You sounded very genuine both of the
times. And somehow, I managed to join both the pieces together
within 10 minutes."

She's listening with her full attention. But she's confused too,
how I find out.

I continue, "So, how do I figure this out? Let me explain… You
told me you had no idea why you said those things at the bar. You
thought maybe it was because you were drunk, and I think you're
right." I nod thoughtfully. "Maybe, because you were drunk, your
old self…who used to flirt and have flings with
strangers…resurfaced. That's why you asked me directly for sex.

But then, when you came back to your senses, you felt regret
because that's not who you are anymore. When I touched your hand,
it triggered bad memories of people from your past, and that's why
you pulled back and told me to leave.

Then 15 minutes later you came outside to apologize thinking
that I was a nice guy and that you had treated me unfairly. But when
I asked more about you, you weren't ready to trust me to tell your
real story. So, you made a fake breakup story." I sigh.

Her eyes are stuck. "Wow! You made me more embarrassed now."

"Please don't be. Being an overthinker isn't a gift," I reply. "But I'm glad that I met you tonight. You're an interesting person I can say."

"But still I'm embarrassed." And with a pause, she adds, "And by the way those 3 months of lockdown I told you about… that's not fake. I became so much addicted to dating apps, so my therapist told me to spend more time with my family. So, I did it… cutting off from my social media… even my friends for 3 months."

Her eyes glistened with tears. "Okay, nice to meet you…?"

"Chetan," I reply. "And your name is?"

"I don't think you need to know my name," she says.

She smiles, turns around, and heads into the pub, carrying her embarrassment with her.

"Okay wait…whatever your name is," I shout. She stops and turns around. "What do you really want from me?" I ask loudly.

I wait for her response, but as usual, she remains silent. Maybe she doesn't have an answer, or perhaps she doesn't trust me enough to share. Or maybe… she's just too afraid to initiate.

I can't see her like this. I never meant to embarrass her for her lies.

I've made my own mistakes and I've lied more times than I care to admit.

So, before overthinking much, the words spill out of me. "Let's date! Like a real date. I know you don't like me… but I know you want intimacy, like really *bad*." Her eyes snap up to meet mine. I continue, "Yeah, what the hell. It'll be a new experience for both of us. Let's see… and what's the worst that could happen? It'll break our hearts? But one day it will gonna happen, right?"

I see her smile through her tears as she slowly walks back toward me.

When she's close enough, she leans in and whispers, "I lied when I said I didn't like you. I think I do. But yes, I want intimacy—just with someone I can trust. Can I trust you, Chetan?"

I smile softly and reply, "And when you asked if I'm loyal, I think I am… unlike your imaginary boyfriend."

She laughs, the sound light and genuine, and then pulls me into a hug.

As she buries her face into my shoulder, she whispers, "Are you really?"

"Yeah," I say softly, holding her closer.

People are noticing us as we've been hugging for a few minutes.

Releasing me from the hug, she says, "Okay, let's date. But there will be one rule."

"What?" I smile, confused.

"Yeah. No sex for three months," she replies.

"What?" I exclaim.

"Yeah. Let's be friends first," she replies.

"Okay. I can do that. Deal."

She smiles. "Yeah, deal."

I extend my hand for a firm handshake, a smile spreading across my face. Our eyes locked.

I don't know how far this will go, but I'm eager to know.

She smiles as she remarks, "Okay… my friend will be here in a few minutes to take me home, so don't get jealous. He's just a friend. I called him when I was drinking to make sure I got home safe."

"Is he really just a friend?" I ask, smiling.

She giggles, "Yeah. Don't worry, no more lies."

I nod. "Okay."

Let's see!

We hold hands, wandering around as we continue to talk.

A little while later, her guy friend shows up, and they start to leave. Before walking out, she turns around, winks at me, and mouths, "Call me." *It's sexy.* She smiles, then turns back around.

I head back inside to grab my bag from the pub. Hugging my bartender friend, he grins and asks, "What? Got lucky tonight?"

"No, but even better," I say with excitement, rushing outside, eager to get home and text the girl who never told me her name, but gave me her number.

I call for an auto-rickshaw, and when it arrives, I get in and tell the driver to take me to Goregaon.

He starts the meter.

But just then, a girl walks up to the taxi and gets in without saying a word.

I think I know her. We met tonight.

Oh yeah! She was the first girl to whom I asked for her name and she told me she had a boyfriend.

I hesitate before asking, "Aren't you the girl who was dancing? The one with a boyfriend?"

"Yeah, I love dancing, and I love people who dance. And I like the way you dance," she replies.

Wait! I know where this is going. I can definitely tell that she's drunk by her tone.

I ask, "Where do you live?"

"Just...nearby," she replies.

"Then why are you taking this taxi? I'm going to Goregaon," I say in frustration.

"No, I'm going to drop you first, then I'll come back. We can talk," I oppose.

The driver is looking at us, confused.

"No, take another taxi," I insist.

"Don't worry, I have a boyfriend. It will just be a friendly chat, nothing more," she replies.

"Look you don't need to drop me. I think you've had too much to drink. Your boyfriend might be worried about you," I advise.

Why isn't she understanding?

"No, he hasn't called me yet," she whispers in her drunk tone, then she falls silent for a moment, then adds, "I want to drop you. It's too late."

"But I'm a guy." I laugh. "Don't worry, I'm safe."

Her eyes narrow as she looks at me. "Alright, you win. I just need to talk to someone right now," she admits, her frustration breaking through.

I look into her eyes and I see a genuine concern.

"Okay," I murmur, the word slipping out before I can think. *I shouldn't have said that. I regret it instantly.*

The auto-rickshaw starts moving.

The girl rests her head on my shoulder, crying softly.

I tap her shoulder, wondering, *"Where am I stuck?"*

She asks, her voice muffled, "Why do boys always do that?"

"What?" I reply, confused.

"First, they beg for love. And when they finally get us, they cheat on us."

"Oh!" I exclaim. "Well, not every guy is like that."

"Yeah, you seem like a nice guy… I feel safe with you." She kisses my cheek and puts her head back again on my shoulder.

'That's not what I meant,' I think.

"What do you do for a living," she asks.

"I work in IT," I reply.

"That's great," she whispers. "Do you have a girlfriend?"

I smile. I take a couple of seconds to answer, "I think I do… but I'm not sure."

"What does that mean?" she asks, whispering.

I glance around the road and realize we need to turn a sudden right, so I command the driver, "Turn right here."

He suddenly swerves, but at the same time, a biker behind us struggles to maintain balance.

The biker somehow manages to avoid falling. He rides up in front of us and yells at the driver, "Motherfucker, can't you see? No indication, no nothing!"

"Hey sorry! it's my fault. I just told him to turn," I say instantly.

"No sir, it's not your fault. It's the driver's fault. He should look around while turning."

"No, no sir. It's my fault," I insist, apologizing.

The girl suddenly lifts her head from my shoulder and says rudely to the biker, "Hey, let's go, bro. We already said we're sorry."

I look at her, and she doesn't seem so drunk anymore.

So, was she acting this whole time?

The biker leaves after how she managed him.

The auto-rickshaw starts moving forward.

"Do you live alone?" she asks her tone now slightly tipsy again.

Yeah, I live alone. But now, I know where this is going. And I don't want to have sex with her. She has a boyfriend, who is cheating on her, and she wants to take revenge by using me.

So, I lie, "No, I live with my family."

"Oh!" she exclaims.

"Yeah."

"Can I come to your place? I feel dehydrated, I think I'm drunk a lot."

I give her my bottle, saying, "Oh, I have water."

"Please turn left," I instruct the driver.

Within five minutes, I've now reached my apartment building.

"This is me," I say to her.

"Are you sure, that I shouldn't come? We can talk more," she insists.

"I can't, sorry. My parents won't allow me to bring any girl at night." I hug her, kiss her forehead, and I get out of the auto-rickshaw. I tell the driver, "Take her home safely."

I lied but I knew that was the best thing to do, and I promised someone that I would be loyal.

I enter my apartment, toss my phone onto the table, and immediately text the other girl I'm seeing.

"Have you reached home?" I type and wait for her response.

After 20 minutes, she replies, **"Thanks for checking in."** I see the typing indicator. She's writing more.

"But I want to ask you something," she texts.

"Sure, but first, tell me your name. I'm dying here, hehe," I reply, trying to lighten the mood.

But her next message wipes away my grin: **"Is she still in your house?"**

I freeze.

"Who?" I type back quickly.

"The girl you left with. Don't lie—I saw her sitting in your cab."

I scramble for an answer.

"Oh, that? She didn't come to my house. She just needed someone to talk to."

Silence.

I send another text. **"I promise you, nothing happened."**

After what feels like forever, her reply comes:

"I don't think you'll ever change, Chetan. I'm sorry I trusted you. Don't text me again."

Panic sets in.

I call her, but she cuts the call.

Before I can try again, my doorbell rings.

At this time? Who could it be?

I walk to the door, my heart racing. Who could it be at this hour?

I unlock it and pull it open.

"Rishi!" *That's unexpected.*

"Rishi? What happened, bro?" I ask terrified because he came from Delhi without telling me, then there must be any reason.

He steps inside, looking drained. "I'm sorry man. Did I disturb you?"

"No man. But is everything alright? You? All of a sudden?"

He sinks onto the couch with a heavy sigh. "No man. Not alright. That's why I came to you. I was missing you."

The living room is dim, so I move to turn on the light, but he stops me. "Please, don't. Don't turn on the lights."

I've never seen him this low in my life, covered in sweat and emotionally shattered.

"What happened, bro? And where is Saloni?" I ask, sitting across from him.

"She's in Canada. We aren't together anymore."

"What? But why? What happened?"

"I don't know, man," he says, his voice trembling. "She's changed." He pauses, staring at the floor before continuing. "Do you remember Lily?"

"Yeah… yeah, I remember. What about her?"

"I need to talk to Lily," he says, his tone desperate.

"But why now? What happened exactly can you tell me?" I ask, my voice rising with frustration.

"I'll tell you and Lily together. Can I call her to your apartment?"

"Is she even in Mumbai?" I ask, confused.

"I don't know where she is. I don't know anything anymore," he admits, his voice breaking. "I'm such a horrible person. I cut her out of my life when she needed me the most. It's karma, bro. It always comes back to you in different ways."

How can I tell him, that I just faced karma a few minutes ago? I never respected the whole dating thing, and when I finally did, it turned its back on me.

I place a hand on his shoulder. "I don't have any problem if Lily comes here."

He looks at me, a glimmer of hope in his tired eyes. "Okay," he says, nodding.

LILY

Timeline: Year 2009-2024

<u>Chapter 1</u>

I think I broke his heart, I should have kissed him. A kiss wouldn't have changed anything. And he's my boyfriend, so I feel guilty right now. What should I do?

I'm an overthinker.

My aunty says, 'Write when you overthink'. Well, I know one person who always writes a journal every day. My boyfriend. I even read his journal in school. He let me read some of them. I think he is so cool because he is writing this cool story about a dragon. I don't know how he thinks so much. It's so obvious that he's an overthinker too.

Maybe I can write my journal too. And I have a diary. I have lots of them from my birthdays, which I never used.

I think it's time.

I go to my cupboard and pick my favorite blue dairy…I lie down on my bed and write:

13th January, 2009

Dear Diary,

This is the first time I'm writing to you. My name is Laveena, also known as Lily, and I live in Jamshedpur. If you're wondering if Lily is my pet name, well, no. Nobody knows me by this name because my boyfriend, my senior in school, gave it to me.

Two months back, one day when I was on the playground with my friends, he came from nowhere handed me a paper, and ran away. When I opened it, there was a poem written on it:

She is like a lily, soft and pure

Her hair is curly, like waves that lure

When I see her, my heartbeat accelerates

Can I get her name?

Well, I know it's a cheesy way to ask a girl's name, but I kinda liked it. So, I wrote, 'Lily for you' on the back of that paper and while going home on the bus I gave it back to him. I went to grab a seat but secretly looked at him, and he was smiling inside.

His name is Rishi, and today we celebrated his birthday at school. I brought a chocolate cake for him which he really liked. So, it was a good day for me today.

But I'm not very happy today. Because he asked for just one thing today which he didn't ask before. When everyone was gone from the cafeteria, it was just me and him. He whispered to me, "Can I get a kiss?" So, I looked around and kissed him on his cheek, and he smiled. But then all of a sudden, he got a little nervous. He became so red. And then he asked, "Can we kiss on the lip?"

That made me nervous too. I never kissed before…like a kiss-kiss. I said, "I think I'm not ready for that."

I could see how disappointed he became after that. He didn't say anything. So, I said, "Sorry, Rishi. But I can't kiss you like that. I'm just not prepared right now."

He shook his head but didn't look at me. He looked at his shoes. I think he got embarrassed. "Don't be sorry, Lily. I think it was too early to ask. I have to go to my class." And he left.

I think he must have thought about this for a long time but didn't get the guts to ask me. And when he did ask, I broke his heart.

I really like him and don't wanna lose him. But I know he's more mature than most guys. I hope he will understand.

A week later…

I am happy that Rishi is coming to my house now. He called me on the phone today, and he didn't sound mad at all. I'm so relaxed. And this is not the first time Rishi coming to my house. My dad loves him, and his dragon story that he's been writing, even the poem he wrote for me.

I'm sorry but I tell everything to my dad. My dad is my best friend, and he's the best dad ever.

20 minutes later, my house bell rings, and I'm in my room, upstairs. But I'm a little nervous now. What if he's coming to break up with me because I didn't kiss him?

I will let Dad open the door.

I hear Dad opening the main door. I'm still in my room. I hear Dad saying, "Welcome my future son-in-law. How is your story going?"

'Really! Future son-in-law? Why Dad? Why?' I think. *I feel a little embarrassed.*

I hear Rishi reply, "Aah, I don't know sir. I'm not sure about this story. I think I will be a writer who writes about real things…Like humans, not dragons. I mean no offense for fantasy but…"

Dad interrupts, "No, it's fine… Wow! That's a great thing son. You are becoming mature… perfect for my daughter." I can sense a quirk in Dad's voice. "Just be yourself and explore…"

I can't hear anything now. Maybe my Dad made Rishi awkward.

But then hear Dad saying, "You can now meet her now."

My dad thinks he's a funny guy.

I can hear footsteps coming from the stairs. I'm nervous.

Rishi knocks on my door.

As I open the door, I hug him tight.

But then Dad shouts, "Doors must be open guys. I'll come and check."

I bet Dad cannot see us from the ground floor.

We laugh softly, and Rishi says, "Your dad's so cool."

"Yeah, I know," I reply.

Releasing me from the hug, Rishi looks into my eyes and says, "Look, I love you, and I'm not just attracted to you. I really love you, Lily… I don't look at you like other guys look at girls in a bad way… You're the most beautiful girl to me and you'll always be, just always remember that."

My God, he is romantic! My eyes melt.

But I still don't feel like kissing him. *What's wrong with me?*

"Do you understand?" he asks smiling.

I nod. "Yeah, a little bit."

He giggles and holds my hands. We sit on my bed. "Lily, I'm just saying it's okay if you're not ready to kiss, you're just 14. We have a whole life for that."

I exclaim, "But you're only 15. And what if I am still not ready after 18?"

He becomes silent and looks at me. "Are you attracted to me?"

"Of course, I'm attracted to you idiot. Otherwise, why would I be with you?"

He's looking down again. I hate when he does that. He might goes to his thinking zone.

"Do I need to kiss you to prove that I love you?" I ask.

"No, no Lily. You don't have to," he replies.

But I can tell his smile is fake—it's all in his eyes.

"What if I insist?" I ask.

I don't know why I said that maybe just to make him happy.

Now his eyes show something, but he's silent.

So, I say, "Okay, you can kiss me, but only for a second… Only touch, not more than that."

"Okay." He blushes.

I can see he's nervous too. He holds my hands and I also can feel his heartbeat, as I think he can feel mine. It's going to be our first kiss ever.

We sigh more than heavy.

He closes his eyes, so I do.

I feel him coming closer, and my eyes automatically open a little. It feels a little uncomfortable, I don't know why.

But then I close my eyes back again.

His lips touch mine, finally, and slowly he goes back. We open our eyes. The kiss was only for a second as I told him.

"Do you like it," he asks.

"Rishi, do you really want my honesty?" I hesitate.

"Yes, yes," he replies quickly.

I take a couple of seconds to reply, "I really think I'm not ready for kisses right now. It's not that you're a bad kisser. It's just that I get a little uncomfortable even thinking about kissing… Is anything wrong with me?" I feel emotional after sharing my truth with him.

He hugs me. "No Lily. It's not a problem. I'm fine with it and I still love you."

I cry. "I promise I'll work on it."

"You'll work with whom you idiot?" He laughs. "Don't take pressure. It's not necessary… I was just curious how it feels to kiss someone… and it felt great to kiss you, even for a second."

I can feel how happy the kiss made him.

Chapter 2

Two months later…

It's 6 am, and I'm all dressed and writing in my diary.

5th March, 2009

Dear Diary,

Today I'm going on a picnic with Rishi and his friends to Maithon Dam. I've heard it's a really pretty place.

It's my first picnic ever! I'm excited.

Actually, Dad never let me go anywhere before, not even with my classmates. But this time, he said yes because of Rishi. He trusts him a lot like his own son, I think maybe also because Rishi doesn't have his parents. My Dad was like, "Go and have fun with your friends."

But they're not really my friends… I only know Rishi.

And Chetan. Ugh, Chetan. He used to hit on me, like, twice. But he doesn't anymore, thank God.

And I don't really know any of Rishi's other friends, but I hope they're nice like him.

To be honest, it's not just Dad who trusts Rishi a lot—I do too. He never makes me feel dumb or weird, even when I act silly. He's different. But sometimes, he's kind of… complicated. Like, even when he's with me, he's off in his own world, thinking about stuff. I guess it's because he's a writer. But honestly, it gets a little boring when he zones out like that. I feel like I should tell him… but maybe I should not. Because when he snaps out of it, he always says something so random and stupid that I can't help but laugh.

Oh! I think they're here. I should go now.

I hear the doorbell, so I rush carrying my backpack.

Opening the door, I notice Rishi take a good look at me. "Hey Lily, you look stunning."

I smile and hug him, kissing him on his cheek. "Come inside."

"No Lily, our friends are waiting in the car, so we have to go now," he replies.

"Oh, Okay," I respond. I step outside, holding hands with Rishi as I shout, "Dad, I'm leaving."

Dad shouts back, "*Okay, my love!* … Rishi, please take care of Lily. She's precious," from the kitchen.

Rishi shouts, "I will sir."

He says to me with a grin, "Your dad also calls you Lily?"

"Just when I'm with you," I respond with a laugh.

We go towards the car passing by the lawn area. I see Chetan sitting in the front row along with a driver. A boy and a girl sitting in the middle row seat. Rishi pulls out the door of the back row for me. I enter, but I'm nervous because I don't know two of his friends who sit in the middle row seat. Rishi shuts my side of the door and he enters from the other side to sit beside me.

"Guys, turn around," Rishi says to his friends. "This is my girlfriend, Lily."

They turn around and pass a smile.

"You've already met Chetan, right?" Rishi asks looking at me.

"Yeah," I reply.

"So, this is Atul and she is…" Rishi says pointing to the boy and the girl in the middle seat. He forgets the girl's name.

"I'm Usha." The girl says and gives a bold smile.

"Hi," I reply. "I've never seen you in school. Are you new?" I ask Usha.

"Oh, I'm from St. Xaviers," Usha replies.

Chetan gasps in enthusiasm. "Yeah, I've heard girls are really hot in Xaviers."

I think Atul doesn't like what Chetan said. "Okay, guys let's move. Driver let's go," Atul commands.

The car moves and the driver turns on the car music, and I instantly feel the fresh morning breeze, so I put my chin on the window. I see the beautiful sunrise, nature, and the birds, and especially the sound of Koel birds singing in harmony.

But I feel everything only for two minutes, and when I turn my face inside, I see Atul and Usha… kissing. And it's not a normal kiss… It's like they have done a course. They are undetachable and so comfortable kissing just in front of us. Suddenly, my eyes go towards Chetan, sitting in the front seat. He's smiling, and his smile is very creepy. He's peeking at them through the mirror.

"Lily. Why are you sweating?" Rishi whispers in my ear.

I take a breath. "Who? Me? No," I say softly.

Rishi smiles. "Relax. We don't have to do this," Rishi says pointing at Atul and Usha. But the car music is a little loud, so they cannot hear what we're talking.

I hold his hand. "Thanks, Rishi," I say looking into his eyes. I go a little close to his ears, and I whisper, "How are they so comfortable around us? They know we are looking at them, right?" Rishi smiled at what I just said. I continue, "And look at your pervert friend Chetan. How he's enjoying looking at them from the mirror."

Rishi's eyes suddenly follow Chetan, and he bursts into loud laughter. And Chetan turns around. But Atul and Usha still don't stir, busy kissing.

Rishi, with his casual wave of his hand, silently communicated, "It's nothing," with Chetan.

Chetan passes a smile to Rishi hinting towards Atul and Usha. Chetan seems like he is feeling proud of Atul.

Rishi whispers, smiling, "They are in love, Lily, and it's their way of showing love."

I nod a little.

It takes me time to think, is this what Rishi also wants? So, I ask, "Is this what you want, too from me?"

He gives me a look for a couple of seconds and he whispers, "Hey relax. I didn't bring you with me to do this. I know it's uncomfortable for you. And I think it's uncomfortable for me too... kissing in front of friends."

"Okay." I nod.

I know Rishi is lying. I just know, because a person like him, who is so romantic, I don't think will hesitate to kiss in public. But I love that he respects my feelings. I hold his hand and put my head on his shoulder and the car is moving towards Maithon Dam.

We're here at the beautiful Maithon Dam, and it's a much better place than I thought. The dam is massive, but it feels safe. I think it would have been much quieter, but there are a lot of people here for picnics. People are playing different games like Antankshari, Dumb Charades, Badminton, and cricket, and few are preparing food. The roads are hilly, mostly and we are tired after exploring the place for half an hour. So, now we decided to sit and just look at this scenic beauty where there's a perfect view of both, the dam and the hills.

I sit beside my favorite person, Rishi. Atul and Usha, sit beside each other.

Chetan. Well, he sits on the other side of Rishi, looking at every girl passing by.

We all look delighted, enjoying the moment.

Looking at me, Usha asks nicely, "How long have you guys been dating?"

"Almost four months?" I reply with a smile.

Usha turns to Atul and she gasps, "Oh!" in surprise.

Rishi and I are confused, looking at each other.

Usha turns again and says, "Sorry guys, in all our trip here, I was only thinking why you guys didn't do a single kiss. But now I understand because your honeymoon period has already ended... Actually, Atul and I've been dating for just 15 days, so we couldn't control ourselves in the car. Sorry if it bothered you guys."

Chetan chuckles, "No, no, it's fine, Usha."

Atul says, giggling, "Babe, their honeymoon period hasn't started yet because they don't do kisses."

I stare at Rishi.

"What?" Usha's confused but smiling.

Atul, Usha, and Chetan start laughing.

Rishi confronts, "Fuck off, you guys."

"Yeah, whatever bro," Atul replies.

"Watch your words," Usha replies to Rishi. "I didn't say any bad words to you."

"You shouldn't have asked that. Lily's younger than us. And what the fuck is the honeymoon period? What are you guys, married?" Rishi blurts to Usha.

I get up and walk straight away to sit somewhere else, not wanting to be part of this fight.

Atul says from behind, "Hey, I'm sorry."

"I'm sorry too Lily if I hurt you, I promise I won't ask that again," Usha says.

But I'm still walking. I actually need some free air.

Chetan says, "Don't stop her Usha, she's crazy sometimes."

I stop.

But then I start walking again.

Wow! Now a creep will decide who I am. My footsteps are much faster now because of this toxicity.

Then, I hear a slap. A tight slap. It must be Rishi.

I stop and turn around; but I see Rishi standing, just behind me. "Lily, stop," he says.

Then who slapped Chetan?

Rishi also turns around to see.

We see Chetan is holding his cheek in his palm.

It's Usha who slapped Chetan. I'm almost 15 feet away from them, but I hear Usha say clearly, "Never call a girl crazy. Remember that."

Chetan nods in embarrassment.

I laugh but I turn back around to walk, but Rishi holds my hand saying, "Lily, they all are immatures. I'm really sorry."

I smile at him. "I know Rishi… I just don't fit in with your friends right now. But I'm not mad at them… especially after that slap."

"Yeah, he deserved it," Rishi says. "And you fit it properly… it's just Usha. I also met her today for the first time."

I interrupt, "It's not her, and I don't hate your friends… I need some air, Rishi… Please go sit with your friends. I'll be back in some moments."

"Are you sure, you'll be fine?" He asks.

"Yeah, just give me some time. I'll be right back."

"Okay," he says and goes back to his friends.

I found a place to sit, where I'm alone and far but I can still see Rishi and his friends from here. And they're still shouting. To be honest I cannot tolerate his friends. They're toxic. I wonder how he made such friends when he's not like them. Especially Chetan. I don't think I can ever be friends with this guy.

I look at the still water of the dam.

I feel so calm and soothing here.

.

.

And suddenly *my eyes catch a glimpse*. A glimpse of a girl who seems like my age. Maybe a little younger, but not much. She has a boy cut hair and she's playing with her dog.

She's the prettiest girl I've ever seen, a little chubby, and with the most beautiful smile. I just can't stop looking at her.

Oh my god! She catches me looking at her. But why am I so nervous?

She passes a smile.

I pass her a nervous smile, and then she goes to her parents.

###

We're back in Atul's car returning home and it's 6:10 pm now. *Everyone's sleeping here*, but I can't stop thinking about the girl I saw.

Her smile was… I cannot forget, it was so bright. And her eyes, so blue.

Am I...?

But I never felt like this for any other girl before. Why only this girl?

I don't feel right.

Should I wake Rishi up?

But Chetan is just beside Rishi now, sleeping. And there's so much silence because there's no music in the car.

I shake Rishi gently trying to wake him up, and I whisper, "Hey Rishi?"

He opens up his eyes, saying, "Hmm."

I whisper, "Can I ask you a question?"

"Yeah, sure," he replies softly.

"No, no, it's very weird. I don't know if you like it," I say after thinking for a moment.

But now he wakes up completely. He says with a smile, "I insist, please, Lily. I won't judge you. I promise."

I hate myself right now to wake him up. I go silent.

"Are you fine? What happens? Is it about them?" he says pointing towards his friends.

"No Rishi, it's nothing," I reply, and I'm nervous.

"Please, Lily. Trust me." He gently put his hand around my shoulder.

I don't know but I think I can trust him.

I hesitate, "Rishi, do you think it's fine if I'm a little bit… you know… just a little bit attracted to a girl?"

"What are you talking about?" Rishi smiles.

"I told you it's weird. It's nothing," I say, smiling.

But then I see Chetan opens his eyes with his same creepy smile, saying, "What? You're… lesbian?"

Rishi opposes, "Chetan, enough."

"You weren't sleeping?" I gasp. My heartbeat rises as I hear Chetan's voice.

"No, we're not sleeping," Atul says and he and Usha turn around smiling.

But I'm embarrassed that everybody heard what I said.

Usha says, "It's normal Lily if you also like girls. It's not a problem, and you should be open and confident about it."

"No, I don't have feelings for girls," I say.

But Rishi interrupts, "For fuck sake, Usha. Don't interfere in my relationship. I have seen enough of you."

I don't know why Rishi reacted that way.

"What the fuck?" Usha yells looking at Rishi in an angry mood. "Don't ever talk to me like that again." She sighs. Atul tries to calm Usha down by rubbing her hand. Usha continues, "And to be honest, I don't think you guys have any relationship. You are just good friends who are pretending to be a couple."

Rishi shouts, "Enough. Don't say any more words. Otherwise…"

I try to calm Rishi down.

What happened to Rishi? I've never seen him this angry. Is this because of me?

Usha gives a sharp look at Atul.

Atul says, "Bro, don't talk to her like that."

"Or what?" Rishi shouts.

"Or get out of my car," Atul says looking straight into Rishi's eyes.

What?

I'm just seeing their faces.

Rishi in anger, says, "Uncle stop the car," to the driver.

"What?" I exclaim. The car stops, and Rishi is getting out of the car in a rush.

"No, no, Rishi. Please don't go," I hold his hand.

But he releases his hand, passes over through Chetan, and exits.

Chetan looks at Rishi, who is outside now. Then Chetan looks at Atul, says, "Shame on you, brother," and gets out of the car too.

But I'm crying. I also want to get out, but my home is far. But Rishi's home is far too.

"Lily, don't worry. We'll drop you home," Usha says.

I don't know what to do. Rishi didn't ask me to come with him. Maybe he wants me to go with Atul and Usha.

The car starts moving and I look at Rishi leaving behind. He's looking at his feet angrily.

Usha continues, "You can share with me whatever you feel inside. I won't judge you like Rishi judges you."

But I'm still looking at him putting my head out of the window. Chetan is saying something to Rishi. They are a little far now.

Usha again says, "Don't worry about them, Lily. They'll reach their homes. They're boys." With a smirk, she continues, "And I've heard that both of their parents aren't alive… So now I guess why they're mannerless."

"Shut up, Usha!" I turn around and shout. "Uncle stop the car." I look at Usha, and say, "And Rishi doesn't judge me. He loves me for what I am."

The car stops, I get out and run towards Rishi.

He looks at me coming, but he still looks angry.

I hug him tightly, and I'm unable to stop myself from crying. But Rishi is silent.

But after a few seconds, Rishi says, "Lily, I think we should take a break, it's not working. And I think you need more time to understand who you actually are."

I release him from the hug. "What?" I whisper. My eyes are wet but I'm confused, what happened to him suddenly?

He continues, "But I'll always be around, I promise whenever you need me. We'll still be friends… and you won't notice a change in me."

My brain freezes, and my eyes just stuck, as I see the emotion in his eyes, they're genuine, and then I realize that he's damn serious right now.

I'm just looking at his beautiful face and every memory of us revolving around my head. Those late-night phone calls, holding hands in the cafeteria, and our first kiss. Everything's going to die soon. I don't know what to do. I also want to beg, so that I can save our relationship.

He continues, "I think it's the best thing to do right now for both of us… We'll see later what we can do."

My tears fall.

"Let's go home, Lily."

CHAPTER 3

2 years later…

I feel sad, so I pen.

15ᵗʰJuly, 2011

Dear Diary,

It's my birthday, and I miss Rishi. It's been two months since he moved to Delhi with his friends to pursue higher studies. But he has stopped calling me now… I don't know why. We were still good friends after the breakup, and he used to come to my house occasionally, never letting me feel alone. He even surprised me on my last birthday by pulling a prank.

But what happened now? Doesn't he miss me?

I want to cry and share my feelings with him. I still regret why I told him that I'm also attracted to girls. I still don't know if I'm straight or gay. Why am I so confused?

My dad still thinks I'm dating Rishi. He asks me about him, and I tell him lies that he's good, and we talk every day on the phone. Maybe if we hadn't broken up, he might have stayed here for me.

I sometimes go to his house to see his grandfather. He's an old man.

I wish Rishi's parents were alive. Maybe then he might have stayed.

I miss him!

I close my diary, putting it aside, and turning off the light.

.

Is he awake? Should I call him? What if he wants *me* to call? Yeah! I should call him.

Taking my phone out from beneath the pillow, I call Rishi.

He picks up. "Hi, Lily."

"Hi, Rishi."

"Are you alright?" he asks.

"Yeah, I'm fine," I reply. "I just miss you."

"I miss you too, Lily. Sorry, I couldn't call you because I didn't have any balance on my phone. I still don't have it. But don't tell my Daadu (grandfather) about this because he's already doing so much for me. I don't want to give him more trouble."

"Don't worry, I will recharge your phone."

"No, no, Lily. You don't have to do this, please. You know you can call me anytime. Incoming calls are free on my phone."

"Okay, forget that… Tell me have you made new friends there apart from your toxic friends," I laugh.

"Yes Lily, I made some," he replies. I can feel the happiness in his voice. "But there's this girl, her name is Saloni. She's very intelligent and we're working on a project together. We're good friends."

"She's just a friend, or your girlfriend?"

"Lily, are you jealous? She's just a friend." He laughs.

"No, why would I be jealous? Have fun."

"What does that mean, 'Have fun.' She's just a friend."

"Then have you tell her about me?"

"Not now. But I'll tell her."

I sigh. "Do you remember what date is today?"

"What date?" he replies.

But then he remembers. "Oh, sorry Lily. Happy birthday, sorry. I'm really sorry."

"Okay, Rishi. I have to go now."

CHAPTER 4

4 years later…

I write…

4th October 2015,

Dear Diary,

Never have regrets… It will only make you weaker. I always regretted in my childhood that I was the reason my mom died after giving birth to me. Relatives still treat me like I'm the sinner of my own family. Well, I don't care anymore.

I too regretted that I could have stopped Rishi 4 years ago from going to Delhi. But when he stopped calling me totally, I understood the hard lesson that you can't hold on to someone…

I know he's not coming back into my life again.

But I don't blame him at all, it's his life.

Well, Rishi is an old story now. And, I'm pretty sure now that I'm attracted to both genders, but mostly girls, and my dad also knows about it. He's cool. We moved to Kolkata last year for my college here. But I still miss Jamshedpur, all those people, and those memories, and whenever I see Rishi's profile on Facebook, I smile. I feel nostalgia. No hard feelings.

And, I have a friend here… well she's more than a friend. Paulomi. I met her just two weeks ago in a bar. Don't judge me, I'm not a child anymore, I'm 19.

Well… She's 35. Again, don't judge me. Nothing's serious between us. She's gorgeous and we are attracted to each other in a way. Not expecting love though… Kinda done with love and all.

Tonight might be the night. My first time with her. Let's see how it goes.

###

I'm at a hotel alone with Paulomi.

"Are you a serial killer, Paulomi? Why are we in a hotel?" I ask, grinning to show I'm joking.

Paulomi hesitates, her expression shifting. "Really, Lily? Not funny," she says, sounding hurt.

"Hey, hey, I'm sorry. You don't even get my jokes," I reply, trying to lighten the mood.

"Yeah, how could I? I'm just an old woman," Paulomi says, her lips twitching with a hint of a smile.

"Hey, hey. I didn't mean that!" I protest.

Paulomi bursts out laughing. "You think only you can crack jokes? I'm not an old woman. Thirty-five is the new twenty."

"Yes, it is," I agree, grinning back.

She sits on my lap on the couch. I lean back, looking into her eyes. They're so sexy. I smile, and she moves closer.

Her hand brushes over my left breast and then rests on my neck. She's caressing it, her touch so soft, so warm. I feel a shiver as her lips press gently against my neck. She takes a deep breath, her lips still on my skin, and I feel a cool breeze. It's so hot.

She looks into my eyes and smiles. "We're in this hotel because I'm renovating my house."

"Okay, I don't care about that right now. Just keep doing what you're doing—it's working. Oh, and get me some wine, if you have any."

She laughs. "Of course, I'll bring you wine."

She turns on some music and heads to the kitchen.

She comes back with two glasses of wine, smiling as she hands me one. She sits on the couch, facing me.

"Hey, by the way, Lily is a beautiful name. Did your dad name you?" she asks.

I take a sip of wine and smile. "Well, it's a long story. My ex-boyfriend gave me that name."

"Oh! That's so sweet. I didn't know you had a boyfriend. Are you still in touch with him?"

"No," I say, shaking my head. "It's been a long time." I pause briefly before adding, "Well, you know enough about me. Tell me about yourself. Are you still in touch with your husband?"

She goes quiet, thinking for a moment. Then, straight-faced, she says, "That was a lie. I never got married. And I don't work in IT. I'm a prostitute."

I burst out laughing. "You got me, babe." I take another sip of wine and look at her seriously. "But I'm not in the mood for jokes now. I want your romance," I say, my voice soft but firm.

Her gaze stays fixed on me. Her expressions remain unchanged.

"You aren't lying, are you?" I ask, my voice trembling slightly.

She shakes her head. "No."

I'm stunned. I put my half-filled glass on the table. I ask loudly, "Why'd you do that? And the big house you told me about?"

"It was a lie too," she says quietly.

"But why? Why, Paulomi?"

She doesn't answer, her eyes avoiding mine.

"I can't stay here with you. Sorry." I stand up quickly, but the room spins. My head feels heavy. I feel dizzy.

"Lily, sit down."

I collapse back on the couch.

"What was in the drink?" I whisper, my voice barely audible. "I wanna go home."

"I'm sorry, Lily," she says, her voice distant, almost mechanical. "But you won't feel a thing."

"What are you talking about?" I whisper, panic rising as I realize I can't feel my body.

"They like you," Paulomi says, her voice cold and detached.

"Who?" I mumble, my words weak as I fall back onto the couch.

My vision blurs. I see two men standing in front of me. Everything fades into darkness.

CHAPTER 5

9 years later...

I wake up to a text.

"Hi Lily,

I know it's been a long time and I don't know if you still remember me. But I still hope you do.

I miss you, Lily. I really do.

I know I don't deserve your attention again, but if it's possible for you, I'd really like to meet you.

I need you, Lily, sorry. I don't have anyone here I can trust because I made the mistake of letting everyone go from my life.

I'm going through a really bad phase right now.

I'm at Chetan's place, in Mumbai. And I'll book you a flight ticket you want to come here.

I'm hoping for your reply, but I'll understand if you don't. Rishi."

.

.

It brings smile on my face after reading the text.

I want to meet him, but I'm unsure what we will talk. It's been so many years. It's not I'm mad at him. I was, but now I'm not, because he didn't do anything wrong. He thought about his career, so he moved to Delhi. There's nothing wrong with that.

He's a good guy.

I have decided that I'm going to meet him, but I need to ask my dad first.

I walk into my dad's room and ask, "Dad, can I go to Mumbai?"

"Yeah, you don't need my permission, honey. It's your life. And you haven't taken a break in a while," he replies, not looking up from what he's doing.

"Dad, it's Rishi."

"Rishi?" he says, suddenly paying more attention. "Our Rishi? What? You guys are getting back together?"

"No, Dad. I told you, I don't want to date anyone."

"Yeah, but he's different."

"He's not different, Dad. We were just stupid kids back then."

My dad stays quiet for a moment.

"Okay, Dad. I'll tell him I'm coming."

As I turn to leave, my dad calls out, "Wait."

I stop at the door. He continues, "Why can't he come here?"

"I don't know, Dad. But I think I should meet him," and after a pause I continue, "and Chetan will be there, too."

"Okay. But how many days are you going for?"

"I don't know, Dad. He didn't tell me."

"Okay, take care, Laveena." He pauses. "You should go. You need a vacation, too."

I turn to leave but he adds, "And stay away from Chetan. I don't know why Rishi is still friends with him."

I write back to Rishi, **"Rishi, I'm coming to Mumbai. And I can book my own tickets... I'm a CA now."**

He writes back, **"Thanks, Lily."**

###

Chapter 6

My flight lands at the Mumbai airport. It's my first time here and my first time traveling by plane. I'm quite excited… and nervous because I'm about to meet Rishi. I don't know what kind of person he is now, but I hope he's the same guy.

Walking through the airport escalator, I see lovers hugging and kissing. I already like this city. I can feel the energy here, so much love and positivity… think I can live in Mumbai.

Finally, I'm in the arrival area, but my eyes are stuck on this beautiful couple, an Indian guy and a white girl, holding hands and walking through the exit. Then suddenly I hear a voice saying, 'Lily'.

It's Chetan. He's standing on the other side of the rope in the arrival hall, smiling. I rush a little toward him and I hug him.

"Long time," I say smiling, releasing from the hug.

He grins and repeats, "Long time my friend."

I playfully cut him, "Whoa! don't think we're friends now just because I hugged you, creepy guy." I laugh.

He looks down, shyly, then puts his hand over his mouth, coughing. "Lesbian Lily," he says with a smirk.

I tap him on the shoulder. "Hey, that's rude." We laugh. "I thought Rishi would come to pick me up."

"Yeah, he's here." Chetan points to Rishi, standing 50 meters away, talking on the phone, facing the opposite direction. "He had to take an important call," Chetan adds.

He looks different… thinner.

Chetan shouts, "Rishi," twice.

Rishi turns around… He catches a glimpse of me. He cuts down his phone and comes towards us. The closer he comes, the clearer I'm able to read his expression. He's carrying a smile, but so much is hidden behind it; It's not the Rishi I used to know.

"How are you, Lily?" Rishi asks softly as he comes close.

I warmly hug him before saying, "I'm good, Rishi."

He looks miserable. He has dark circles… and he's definitely hiding something inside. Maybe that's why I'm here.

Rishi says, "Let's go guys."

"So, Rishi, do you want to tell me anything?" I finally ask. We're sitting in Chetan's 2 BHK apartment, feeling a little drunk now.

"It's nothing, Lily. I was just missing you both," Rishi replies, smiling, his tone clearly slurred.

"I don't think it's nothing, bro. Come on, you can tell us," Chetan insists.

I interrupt, "It's fine, Rishi. You can tell us later. Let's just enjoy this time."

"Yeah, guys. I'm having a great time with both of you. Let's not ruin the moment," Rishi says, nodding. "So, Lily, how's your life?"

I look at Rishi, the
n glance at Chetan, who's covering his mouth, smiling. This is the third time Rishi's asked me that tonight. He's definitely too drunk. I think it's his 7th drink, and I'm on my 3rd.

"You didn't say, Lily. How's life?" Rishi repeats, slurring the words.

"Life's good, Rishi. Life's good. I think you should go to sleep now. You've had enough for today," I reply, hoping he'll let it go.

"Why? I'm enjoying it… Don't you want me to stay, too?" Rishi says, a sly smirk crossing his face.

I pause, confused by his words. Why did he say that? I think to myself. I glance at Chetan, who's silent now.

I lean toward Chetan and whisper, "Tell me, what happened to him?"

Chetan whispers back, "He's going through a breakup. But he didn't tell me exactly what happened."

Oh, poor Rishi. I feel for him, maybe because I'm a little drunk too. Without thinking, I go over to him and hug him tight.

Rishi goes quiet for a moment, but then he laughs softly. "What, Lily? I'm fine. Nothing happened to me."

I keep holding him, and after a beat, he wraps his hands around my back gently. "You know what, Lily? I never thought you would come to see me. You're still the nicest and most beautiful person I used to know. You're not like me."

I whisper, "You're nice too, Rishi…"

Rishi interrupts, his voice low and heavy. "I wish I'd never left Jamshedpur… my life would've been different. Getting older with you would've been different. I don't deserve you, Lily. I don't deserve you."

His words hit me hard, and I can feel the genuine emotion in them. I stay silent, unsure of what to say.

"Guys, I'm here, too!" Chetan suddenly jumps in, wrapping his arms around both of us in a group hug.

We pull away from each other after a minute of silent hugging. Chetan beams, a big smile on his face. "That felt great," he says.

Rishi looks up at Chetan, his expression suddenly serious. Out of nowhere, Rishi asks, "Do you know, bro, what exactly it takes to write a book?"

Chetan's expression shifts, and I can see he's confused. I feel the same way, wondering if it's just another random drunk thought from Rishi.

"Story?" Chetan replies, still unsure.

Rishi answers, his voice a little more intense now, "Soul… time… energy. And she wanted me to change the scenes."

Chetan looks even more lost. "What are you talking about?" he asks, clearly puzzled. Then he guesses, "Who? Saloni?"

"Saloni," I repeat, trying to recall where I've heard that name before.

"Saloni," Rishi sighs. His mood shifts instantly, and he starts staring blankly at the wall. He continues, his voice quieter now, "Saloni moved to Canada six months back. We had a small fight before that... A few days after she left, she started ignoring my calls and messages, saying she had a lot of work. And after two months, she just stopped calling. I didn't know what to do to get her back. So, the only thing that came to my mind was to write a novel about me and her. I started writing, and every day, I felt like she was still with me in my words. I thought that someday she'd call. But she didn't... I finished the novel this month, after four and a half months. I published it. I even texted her to read it. And she read it."

"Then?" I ask, my curiosity piqued.

Chetan and I both look at Rishi, his gaze still fixed on the wall.

Rishi finally speaks, his voice quiet. "She didn't like the book. She told me it's unprofessional to write someone's story without their permission. She even asked me to change the scenes that were... intimate between us."

"Did you use her real name?" I ask, wanting to understand the situation better.

"No," Rishi replies.

"Did you write anything that could defame her?" Chetan asks.

"No, why would I do that? You know I love her," Rishi responds, a hint of frustration in his voice.

"But you still need permission to write their true story," I point out.

Rishi turns to me. "But I loved her, Lily… and it was my story too."

I take a deep breath, trying to help him see the bigger picture. "Maybe she doesn't love you anymore… or maybe she's with someone else right now," I say. "Wake up, Rishi! Love isn't everything."

Rishi nods slowly. "Yeah, you're right."

"So, did you change the scenes?" Chetan inquires.

Rishi sighs, shaking his head. "No."

Chetan nods, his expression softening. "Yeah, good. It's your decision. It's your book."

Rishi continues, his voice barely above a whisper, "No, I unpublished the novel from everywhere."

Chetan and I both gasp in disbelief.

"What?" Chetan shouts, his voice rising with frustration. "It's your book, not hers. Why would you do that?"

Rishi looks down, almost ashamed. "Actually, I wrote the book for her. It's fine she didn't like it, at least she has the book now."

Chetan's frustration boils over. He practically yells, "Are you insane, man? Open your eyes, she doesn't give a fuck about you anymore. So, don't be so nice!"

Rishi remains silent, his eyes staring at nothing.

I break the silence, my voice calm yet firm. "I don't think he's insane. He chose to unpublish, instead of changing the scenes. He took a stand for his art, for which he invested so much time. If he had changed those scenes, the whole book wouldn't have made any sense. It would be soulless… garbage."

Chetan interrupts, his tone sharp. "Then he didn't have to change anything. He should've ignored her, just like she ignored him… But unpublishing the book?"

I sigh, shaking my head. "Okay, leave him alone now," I say, my voice softening as I turn to Rishi. I rub his shoulder gently.

"I don't know if I can write again," Rishi says, his voice low and uncertain.

Chetan, frustrated, shakes his head. "Oh, come on, man. You'll forget her. Just give it some time."

Rishi pauses, thinking deeply. "I only took validation from her for my books. She liked all the books… but she didn't like the one I wrote for her."

Chetan laughs bitterly. "That's ironic."

"Enough, Chetan, fuck off," I snap, my patience running thin.

The room falls into silence for five long seconds.

Then, Rishi speaks quietly, almost to himself. "I think I'm lost."

"Aren't we all lost, Rishi?" I say, frustration lacing my words.

Chetan raises an eyebrow, giving me a look.

"I think I'm gonna throw up," Rishi mutters before rushing toward the bathroom.

Chetan turns to me, his voice low with curiosity. "What was that, Lily? How are you lost?"

"Nothing. It just came out of my mouth."

I quickly follow Rishi to the bathroom.

Chapter 7

Next day…

My sleep breaks at 9 am when the sunlight starts to hurt a little. I think I like Mumbai's weather, it's not really cool and not really hot. Maybe I'll move to Mumbai one day. I can get a lot of opportunities, after all, it's called a city of dreams. I can also bring my Dad here, but I don't know if he agrees. But I can't leave him alone in Kolkata. If he doesn't agree, then I'll have to stay with him.

I wake up, yawning. I sit up on the master bed of Chetan's apartment. Suddenly my eyes notice a small photo frame, which is lying on a wooden table. I go near it and take it in my hand.

It's a picture of the five of us: me, Rishi, Chetan, Usha, and Atul from the day we went to Maithon dam together. *How sweet of Chetan.* We look so young in this picture. I remember how fun that day was. How they fought like kids that day over little things.

I remember how I met my first girl crush that day, that boycott hair. It brings a smile to the face.

Then I remembered that was the same day when Rishi and I broke up.

Well, it makes me sad, and also think that things might have been different if Rishi didn't leave Jamshedpur, but I think everything happens for a reason.

What if he didn't go to Delhi, then? He could never have met Saloni, the girl with whom he was with for 8 years.

What if he would have stayed in Jamshedpur? Then maybe I could have broken his heart in some way. I would never want that for him.

I still love him and I'm glad he got a reason to call me again. I know for sure he doesn't love me anymore.

But I have no bitter feelings for him, he didn't do anything wrong with me. He was a true gentleman from the start.

I'm overthinking again, I think I should write it down.

I see my purse sitting on the table, so I search for my diary inside the purse. But I can't find it.

That's strange.

I ask a bit loud, "Rishi… Chetan… Have you guys seen my diary?"

But I haven't gotten any response from them. So, I go to the living room, but I cannot find them, and not the diary. I go check on another bedroom, but they're not here too.

Then I hear the shower running from the bathroom, I ask, "Rishi, are you inside?"

"No, it's me," Chetan replies.

"Have you seen my diary?" I ask.

"He replies, "No Lily, why do you always think that I'm a bad guy? I don't read anyone's diary."

It makes me nervous now. So, I ask, "Where's Rishi?"

"I don't know. I haven't seen him, I just woke up now… Maybe he went outside," Chetan replies.

"Okay."

I go to each room again, but I'm unable to find my diary.

But then I see the shadow like someone is sitting on the balcony. I go near and it's Rishi facing opposite.

I ask, "Rishi, have you seen my diary?"

Rishi doesn't respond.

I ask again, "Rishi?" tapping his shoulder from behind, and then suddenly my eye catches a glimpse of my diary.

I yell in front of Rishi, "How dare you read my diary?"

But I see his face, stunned.

Then I look at my diary.

That page opened was my real nightmare, which I never told anyone about. Only my diary knew.

How could you be so careless, Lily? I ask myself, without saying.

He's mad and doesn't look at me while asking, "Lily, you were?"

"Stop." I immediately interrupted him. "Don't say that word. I hate it."

He didn't look at me while asking. I can say he's mad.

My heartbeat rises so fast. I don't know how to respond, and I can't control myself from crying. Rishi holds my hand and rubs my palm. I sit down and can't stop myself from hugging him. I cry louder.

He says, "It's Okay Lily, don't stop yourself," tapping my back.

I cry because the scariest moment comes before my eyes. It didn't happen in front of my eyes, because I was drugged at that time and was unconscious. But I still remember those two faces before I faded away. I don't think I'll ever forget those faces.

I remember I woke up in the middle of the night, and everyone was gone from the hotel room, I had no clothes on and I was alone hurting badly. I had no idea how to get home. I somehow managed to put my clothes on and run.

And I'm still running from the thought of why I went to that hotel.

I never talked to anyone about this. Not even my dad.

And after that day I'm not the same person. But I'm proud of what I have become.

It's been half an hour; everything is silent. I *open* my eyes and see Chetan sitting beside us. I release myself from the hug with Rishi.

Rishi looks at me with full attention, and asks, "Lily, if you want to talk about that…"

I interrupt, "Yeah, but not now."

"Okay, okay," Rishi replies.

I like this silence between the three of us when we're sitting together and not expecting anything.

Rishi breaks the silence. He holds my hands, and with sincerity in his eyes, he says, "Lily, I promise you I will not leave you again on your own… I promise. You will never feel alone." I can see how genuine he sounds.

"Rishi, you shouldn't have read my diary," I whisper.

"I had to Lily, I had to. Because when I asked you yesterday about 'How's life', you didn't respond. Then I knew there was something wrong." He continues after a pause, "Lily, I know I don't love you like when we were kids, but I also know that the respect I have for you now is more than love… And you deserve much more than me."

"Don't worry Rishi, we all are on the same page," I say smiling, wiping my tears.

CELEBRATION

Timeline: Year- 2027

Chapter 1

Usha enters the house, her mood heavy. She tosses her purse onto the couch and heads to the kitchen for water. But the sight of dirty dishes in the sink halts her. With a bitter sigh, she rolls up her sleeves and starts cleaning. Once done, she puts food on the dining table, and without taking any bite, she heads to the bedroom, drained.

Atul walks in shortly after, setting his bag aside. He notices his dinner on the dining table, sits, eats in silence, then moves to the kitchen. After rummaging in the fridge for a moment, he goes to the bedroom, where Usha lies facing away from him in the dark. He asks, "Ush, do you want ice-cream? I'm ordering."

She doesn't respond, her eyes wide open but fixed on the wall, not acknowledging him.

Atul assumes she's asleep. He quietly leaves, closing the door behind him, and orders the ice cream while flipping on the TV. Almost twenty minutes pass before he returns to the bedroom.

He slips into bed, reaching out to spoon her, his hand resting gently on her arm. Smiling, he closes his eyes.

"Do you think this is working between us?" Usha's voice, soft but clear, breaks the silence.

Atul's eyes snap open. Usha slowly turns to face him, her gaze piercing through the dim light.

"Wow, I thought you were asleep," he says, startled.

Her eyes remain fixed on him, waiting.

The smile fades from his face. "What do you mean?" he asks, forcing a light chuckle.

She studies his expression, then sighs. "You know what… it's late. Let's talk tomorrow." She starts to turn away.

"No, no." He gently grabs her arm, stopping her. "What's on your mind? Tell me."

She hesitates, looking down before speaking again, her voice softer now. "Do you think we should keep going like this?" She looks up into his eyes, her brow furrowed. "I mean... there's no romance left between us, Atul. Sometimes we barely even talk. Is this how we're supposed to live for the rest of our lives?"

Her words hang in the air. He doesn't respond right away, lost in thought.

She reaches out, brushing her hand through his hair as she moves closer. "It's not that I don't love you," she whispers. "I always will. But... the spark? It's gone, Atul. Our marriage feels... hollow." She pauses, a sad smile tugging at her lips. "What do you think?"

He nods slowly, still processing, as if unsure how to respond.

Seeing his struggle, she continues, trying to lighten the moment. "Look, I know you feel it too. You're just too shy to admit it, to make a move. But it's not such a big deal. People here celebrate divorce."

His heartbeat rises after hearing the word 'divorce', but he expressionless.

She continues, "We're not in India anymore. Nothing will really change. We'll still be in each other's lives... but with more freedom."

Her eyes search his face, waiting for some response.

Finally, his eyes meet hers and he speaks, "Okay... if this what you want."

Chapter 2

A few hours before the divorce talk (Usha's POV) …

I stand back, wiping the sweat from my forehead with the back of my hand, a streak of blue paint smudging across my skin. My painting is finally done.

I'm Usha, and I live in Brampton, Canada, with my husband, Atul. I've spent years dedicated to my art. Painting has always been my escape, a way to channel the emotions I can't always put into words.

"Wow, Usha, that's amazing!"

I don't need to turn to recognize Noah's voice. He's always hanging around after hours, charming in that casual way he has, like the world's never really pressing on him the way it does on me. I can hear him coming closer, and I feel his presence even before he's standing next to me, looking at the canvas. He's much younger than me, by at least ten years, but he carries himself with a kind of confidence I can't help but notice.

I offer a small smile, still focused on the painting. "Thanks, Noah. It took longer than I expected, but it's finally done."

His laugh is soft, almost teasing. "You're way too modest. We're all just trying to keep up with you."

I pass him a smile.

I feel him move closer, his body warmth radiating toward me. I should step away, and create some space… but I don't. There's a tension in the air, one I've felt before, but never let myself acknowledge until now.

"You've got a little paint…" His hand reaches out before I can react, his fingers brushing gently against my temple. The touch lingers just a moment too long, and my breath catches, but I don't move.

His eyes are locked on mine, and I feel something shift between us, something I've tried to ignore for weeks. I should step back. I should say something.

But I don't. I don't know why.

Instead, I let the silence stretch, thick and heavy. His fingers trail down from my temple, grazing my cheek, and my heart pounds in my chest.

I turn to face him fully now, intending to say something—anything—but before the words form, his lips are on mine.

I freeze for a second, shocked more by my own lack of resistance than by the kiss itself.

I don't push him away.

Instead, I kiss him back.

It's a simple kiss at first, almost innocent, but it deepens quickly. His hands are on my waist, pulling me closer, and I find myself responding to him, the intensity of it all taking me by surprise. My body reacts before my mind can catch up.

"Noah, we need to stop," I manage to whisper, pulling back slightly, just enough to catch my breath. My heart is racing, but not just from the kiss—it's racing from the guilt, from the realization of what I'm doing. "I'm married. I have a husband," I say.

But Noah doesn't pull away. He looks at me, his eyes darkened with desire. "Does it really matter right now?" His voice is low… but wild.

My mind screams that yes, it matters. Of course, it matters. I'm a married woman. I love my husband. Don't I?

But my body… my body is betraying me. Noah's hands move to the small of my back, pulling me closer again. His lips find my neck, trailing soft kisses down to my collarbone, and I feel my resolve slipping, piece by piece.

I try to say something, but the words die on my lips. His touch is intoxicating, and for the first time in years, I feel… alive—desired in a way I haven't been in so long.

"Noah, we shouldn't…" I shout.

But even as I say it, I'm not stopping him. His fingers slip under the hem of my shirt, the warmth of his touch sending shivers down my spine. I gasp softly, closing my eyes as he lifts me onto the edge of the table, his body pressing against mine.

There's a moment—a brief, fleeting moment—where I could stop this. I could push him away, gather my things, and leave. I could go back to the life I've built with my husband.

But I don't.

Instead, I give in.

The studio is quiet now, except for the sound of our breathing, our hurried movements, the soft rustle of clothing being shed. My mind is racing, torn between the weight of my actions and the overwhelming sensations coursing through my body. I don't think about what comes next. I don't think about anything except this moment, this overwhelming need that's taken hold of me.

It's only afterward, when the room falls into a tense silence, that the reality of what I've done crashes down on me. Noah is lying next to me, his arm resting lightly on my stomach, but I can't bear to look at him.

I stare up at the ceiling, my heart pounding in my chest. The guilt settles in almost immediately, like a heavy weight pressing down on me.

What have I done?

I've been faithful to my husband for so many years, and now… now everything has changed.

I carefully slip out from under Noah's arm and quickly gather my clothes, my movements rushed and anxious. My hands shake as I dress, the weight of my actions pressing harder and harder with each passing second.

Noah stirs but doesn't say anything. I don't look back at him. I can't. I need to get out of here, away from the mess I've created.

The cool night air hits me as soon as I step outside, and I breathe it in, trying to steady myself. I walk quickly, my mind racing. What am I going to do? How can I face my husband after this?

###

I'm home, and Atul's still not here. Oh, thank God, I'm exhausted. I throw my purse on the couch and head to the kitchen. The sink is full of dirty dishes, staring at me like they always do. I start cleaning them, but my mind is elsewhere. The guilt.

But I also think, *Is this what I'm going to do for the rest of my life? Clean dirty dishes? Is this what I'm made for?*

I'm mad at me, but also at my life right now.

I'm an artist—a renowned one. I have money. I should be independent. I tell myself I am, but why don't I feel it? Sure, there's guilt gnawing at me. I did something terrible today, something I never thought I'd do. I betrayed Atul. But the strange thing is, I felt alive today for the first time in so long. Not because of Noah, not because now I like him. I don't. And it's not that I love Atul any less. He's a great husband. There's nothing wrong with him.

Today wasn't about Noah or Atul. It was about me.

I leave the dishes half-done, place some food for Atul on the dining table, and drag myself to bed. I don't feel like eating. The guilt alone is enough to fill my stomach. I pull the blankets around me, but I can't sleep. My mind is racing.

Today, I realized something I've been avoiding for years—I can't be this person anymore. I need my own space, my own privacy. Maybe someday, I'll have desires, real ones, and I'll go after them without guilt. I'll be my own boss. No expectations. No compromises.

But how do I approach Atul? What's his fault in all of this? He hasn't done anything wrong. I did. I'm the one who betrayed him. How can I even think about staying with him when I'm hiding something like this?

I don't know how he's going to react if I ask for a divorce. The word feels heavy, but I know now that it's what I need. I can't live like this, in this lie, pretending everything is okay when it's not. I've already crossed a line.

I'm sure of it now. I have to ask him. Somehow. It's the only way.

I can't live like this anymore.

Chapter 3

A few hours before the divorce talk (Atul's POV) …

I sit at my desk, tapping my pen against the stack of papers in front of me. Work feels slow today. I glance at the clock—still, an hour left before lunch.

The idea of leaving here for a while sounds nice, but I can't help feeling that even lunch won't help me escape this low mood. My thoughts keep drifting to Usha. I wonder if she's busy with her painting if she's still feeling as distant as she has lately. It's been harder to connect, but I don't know how to fix it.

I'm still lost in thought when I hear footsteps approaching. I look up to see Shalini walking toward me, a soft smile on her face. She's always been friendly, but there's something different in her expression today.

"Hey, Atul," she says, her voice warm. "I was about to head out for lunch and thought… maybe you'd like to join me?"

The offer takes me by surprise. I hadn't really spoken to Shalini much beyond the usual office banter, but here she was, standing there, casually asking me out for lunch. There's a spark in her eyes, a kind of playful energy. I can't lie—it feels nice to be noticed like that.

I hesitate, glancing at my computer, then back at her. Lunch with her? What would Usha think? It's not like it would mean anything—it's just a meal, after all. But then I think of Usha again, of the quiet mornings we've spent together lately, the way she's been so absorbed in her painting, the way she sometimes smiles at me when she doesn't think I'm looking. Even when things feel distant, I know we have something solid.

"Lunch?" I repeat, stalling.

Shalini's smile widens. "Yeah, just a quick bite. There's a new place I've discovered, it's Chinese. I figured it'd be better than eating alone."

For a second, I consider it. There's a part of me that's curious, maybe even tempted. She's attractive and confident, and it's been a while since anyone has made me feel that kind of attention. But then, in my mind, I see Usha.

I take a breath, then shake my head, offering Shalini a small smile. "I appreciate the offer, but I've got a lot of work to catch up on. Maybe another time."

She looks a little surprised but covers it with a shrug. "All right, no problem, Atul. Next time maybe," she says, flashing me one last smile before turning and walking away.

I watch her go, feeling relief.

5 hours later...

I get into my car and turn the engine on, but my thoughts are still on that moment. I could've gone, could've made a new friend.

Before I can let myself get too deep into my thoughts, my phone rings, pulling me back to reality. It's Rishi.

Rishi!

A nostalgic breeze of excitement runs through me.

Rishi's my childhood buddy, and this call I get from him... maybe after 3 years, I don't even remember.

Hitting the button on the dashboard to answer, I shout, "Bro, what's up?"

"Hey, man. I'm great. Actually, I'm in Canada," he replies.

"What the fuck! You're here," I shout with enthusiasm. "Let's meet then."

"I'm sorry, man. I have a flight back to India tonight. I was only here for my new book release and thought I should give you a call."

"But still, we can meet, right? We have enough time," I inquire.

He's quiet, but then breaks his silence. "Actually, I have to meet someone else." And with a soft laugh he continues, "Someone more important."

I laugh. "What the fuck man. Then why'd you call me?" I inquire.

"Sorry man. You are a great friend, and we can meet anytime later we know that. But I can't meet this person again."

"Who?" I say, confused. I think who lives in Canada is more important than me... definitely not Usha, because Rishi and Usha can't survive alone in the same room for more than 10 minutes. They've always fought like kids over small things.

Then who?

"Oh! Saloni?" I ask eagerly.

Obviously, who else could be? The bastard didn't reply and might be shying right now that I guessed it right.

But I suggest, "Bro, don't go that road again, she doesn't deserve you... You have a much better career than her. And you can get any other girl. Why her, man? She left you for her career."

He breaks his silence. "Just last time bro, I only want to see her if she's happy. Just give me her address."

I interrupt, "Yeah I don't have any problem, but you know she has a boyfriend, right?"

He takes a couple of seconds to say, "Really?"

"Yeah," I answer. "Do you still need her address?"

He hesitated, "I mean if I'll get time before my flight..."

I interrupt, "Okay, she will be at her office right now. I'll text you her office address. But just watch her, don't go and talk with her. And if any chance you get caught by her, don't tell her that I gave you her address... Saloni and Usha are very good friends, you know that. And I don't want any misunderstanding with my wife right now."

He replies, "I promise I won't talk to her. I'll just watch her." He continues, "But promise me too that if you meet Saloni, you won't tell her that I was in Canada."

"Okay."

"Thanks, man... for understanding. Bye." He disconnects.

Such a loser. What does he see in this girl?

I enter my house, putting the bag down, and I see dinner on the dining table.

That's strange. Is she mad?

I eat dinner and think, 'What I've done wrong now?'

I should buy ice cream for her.

Chapter 5

Five days have passed, and it's the night of the divorce celebration. Usha and Atul have invited their close friends—Saloni, her boyfriend Miguel, and Meghna with her husband Rahul—over to their home. The six of them sit around the dining table, glasses of wine in hand, surrounded by balloons and soft lights. The atmosphere is strangely celebratory for the occasion.

Saloni raises her glass with a bright smile. "To the new life of Usha and Atul."

Everyone clinks their glasses and cheers.

"So, what's next?" Saloni asks, her eyes glinting with curiosity.

"I've already found a new apartment," Usha replies, surprising everyone.

"You have?" Atul turns to her, raising his eyebrows.

"Yeah," Usha responds, smiling softly. "I mean, I can't stay here forever."

"You don't have to rush, though," Atul says, a hint of concern in his voice. "I'll help you find a better place. No need to settle."

"Aww, you guys are too sweet," Miguel chimes in, squeezing Saloni's hand.

Saloni chuckles, leaning in to kiss Miguel. "Yes, babe, they are."

Atul watches them with a sad smile, his eyes betraying the emotions he's trying to keep hidden. Saloni, noticing his expression, gives him a brief glance of sympathy.

"What about you, Atul?" Saloni asks, breaking the brief silence. "What's next for you?"

Atul hesitates for a moment, then shrugs. "I don't know... I'm thinking of going back to India for a while, to visit my father."

"That's a good idea," Usha nods, her tone supportive but detached.

Atul rubs his temples, his face suddenly clouding. "Guys, I've got a headache. You all should enjoy yourselves, but I need to lie down for a bit."

"Come on, bro, don't leave us now," Rahul protests. "Stay a little longer."

Atul forces a smile but shakes his head. "Sorry bro, I really need some rest."

He stands and heads to his room, leaving the others to continue their conversations. After a few minutes, Saloni excuses herself and follows him.

She knocks gently on his door before pushing it open. Atul is lying on the bed, scrolling aimlessly through his phone. He looks up as she enters.

"I knew you just made an excuse to leave the table. This party is a drag, anyway," Saloni says, a teasing smile on her lips.

Atul chuckles weakly, setting his phone aside. "It's not exactly the kind of celebration I ever imagined."

Saloni sits on the edge of the bed, her expression softening. "Atul, I can tell you're not okay with this divorce. You don't have to pretend. It's written all over your face."

Atul's smile fades, and he looks down at his hands. "Yeah... I guess I'm not ready. Usha pushed for this celebration. It feels... wrong."

"I get it," Saloni sighs, shaking her head. "Usha's my friend, but I know she can be... a bitch. I can't believe she convinced you to go through with this party."

Atul stays silent for a moment, his thoughts clearly far away. Finally, he speaks, his voice barely a whisper. "Saloni, can I ask you something? And please, don't take this the wrong way."

"Of course. Anything," she replies, her gaze steady.

Atul looks at her intently, his eyes searching hers. "Do you ever miss Rishi?"

The question hangs in the air for a moment, and Saloni's face hardens slightly. She doesn't answer right away, the silence between them growing heavier.

Atul, sensing her hesitation, continues gently, "You should read his books, you know."

Saloni scoffs lightly. "I don't have time for that..."

Atul cuts her off, his voice firmer now. "Make time. Try to find yourself in them. Even the non-fiction. It's been three years since you broke up, but I don't think he's ever gotten over you."

Saloni shifts uncomfortably, her eyes flicking away from his. Atul sighs, his tone softening again.

"Usha and I used to laugh about how much of a loser Rishi was, back then. But now... I feel for him. Maybe I understand him better. Maybe... Rishi and I are in the same place now."

Saloni bites her lip, clearly unsure of what to say.

Chapter 6

Atul's been back in Mumbai, India for a week now, living with his father. The house is the same—familiar smells, familiar sights.

But he feels bored.

Atul calls Rishi and tells him he's divorced and has finally moved back to India. Rishi, in shock, tells Atul to meet him at Versova Beach at 6 p.m. the evening.

***

It's almost sunset, and Atul and Rishi sit quietly at the beach watching the soothing tides roll in, without exchanging a word.

Rishi breaks the silence. "You know Atul, this is where I used to come once in a while after Saloni left."

"Yeah man, it's really peaceful in here," Atul replies, looking at Rishi. "Do you wanna talk about Saloni?"

Rishi smiles. "No… I think I got my closure in Canada. Thanks to you, man. She's happy."

Rishi changes the subject and asks, "By the way, how long are you staying in India?"

"I'm not sure, man. Maybe I'll stick around," Atul replies. "You know my dad's alone, and he's getting old."

"That's good to hear," Rishi says with a nod. "He needs someone to be there for him, and I think you're the best company he could have right now."

Atul nods with a smile and looks straight at Rishi. "You know, last night my dad and I had beer together for the first time and we had a deep conversation about life… He feels like a friend now," he says.

"That's awesome, my boy! Finally—drinking with Dad, that's the dream," Rishi exclaims, his eyes lighting up.

"Yeah, it really is," Atul agrees, his smile growing wider.

Rishi says, "And, I also think he's lucky to have you as a son. I mean look at you. You're financially stable at 33…And you're divorced too at this young age. You have seen everything, man."

Atul's expression turns sad, but Rishi doesn't notice. After a moment of silence, Atul says quietly, "You know, sometimes I regret going to Canada when my mom begged me not to… and now she's gone."

Rishi says, "Hey, don't blame yourself for that. It's not your fault."

Atul sighs. "I just regret not spending more time with my parents."

Rishi places a hand on his shoulder. "Look, everything happens for a reason. And didn't you just say you and your dad are like best friends now? So enjoy this moment, my friend."

Atul nods slowly. "Yeah, you're right."

They continue staring at the same view for a few more minutes until Atul lights a cigarette.

Watching him, Rishi asks, "Hey, can I ask you something?"

"Yeah, go ahead," Atul replies.

"Do you talk to your cigarette?" Rishi asks with a smile.

Atul laughs. "What kind of question is that?"

Rishi chuckles awkwardly. "Nothing, I'm just writing something about a cigarette."

Atul thinks for a moment, then says, "I mean… maybe? Actually, I don't get your question. How can a cigarette talk back to you?"

Rishi leans forward slightly. "No, the cigarette isn't talking back. It's just a way to talk to yourself, you know? Like, really deep conversations with yourself. But sometimes, I think it's dangerous to get to know yourself that closely."

Atul gasps, "Oh!" Then he laughs. "Yeah, I think I talk to my cigarette, too. You writers are crazy, though. Why do you always have to make simple things sound so fancy?"

Rishi laughs. "What! 'Talking to a cigarette' sounds cool."

"Yeah, it does," Atul admits with a grin.

They both share the same cigarette and then Rishi says in enthusiasm, "Hey, let this be our last cigarette. What say?"

Atul bursts out laughing. "You know how many times we've said that? By the way, where's Chetan? I forgot to ask."

Rishi smirks. "That motherfucker is in Bali, enjoying his honeymoon."

Atul's eyes widen. "What the fuck? He's married? I can't believe ii.

Rishi shrugs dramatically. "Yep, my best friend's a changed man now."

MEET

Timeline: Year 2028

<u>Chapter-1</u>

I'm Rishi. It's 3 a.m. I've been deep in my new book when my phone buzzes. A message lights up the screen, and I freeze. It's from Saloni.

Saloni.

The text reads, **"Hey, I'm back in India. Can we meet?"** I can hardly believe it.

'Why?' I think. 'Why now?'

But why do I feel good too? I have no control over my emotions right now.

Saloni—my college girlfriend. We spent eight years together, right until 2024, when everything fell apart.

And now it's 2028. Four years of silence. How does someone find the nerve to send a text like that after all this time? Why now? If we walked away, if we decided to let go, why reopen those old wounds?

Maybe it's because I'm rich now. Maybe she's curious about the cars, the lavish lifestyle that comes with being a prominent writer. She always said she was attracted to power. But Saloni never seemed like the type to care about money, at least not back then. So why reach out now? What's the catch?

To be honest, I'm mad. Four years and she drops a message like nothing happened. But at the same time, I feel... good. I hear from her. I know she's a little too late, but I'm not bitter. I don't have any expectations left from her.

Or do I? Do I still have feelings for her? I don't even know. But yeah, I have everything now—everything she ever wanted. I could give her the world, buy her anything. It's just ironic that I'm finally in a position to give her what she used to dream about... and now she's reaching out.

I'm not even sure anymore. Because when she left me, I was just a wannabe writer. She moved to Canada with her family and stopped talking after a while. I wrote an entire novel about us to show her how much I loved her. She didn't appreciate it. She just... faded away.

That was the hardest part—trying to keep loving someone who wasn't there anymore. I held onto a version of her that didn't exist. She never told me it was over. She just drifted out of my life like a ghost. It hurt, not having closure, not knowing if I should move on. I thought maybe one day she'd wake up, text me, and things would be different. But that never happened.

And now, four years later, she sends a message. I don't trust her anymore.

I loved her. I was sure I'd marry her someday. We talked about it. We even talked about having kids.

But guess what? I'm not that guy anymore. I'm always writing now, busy with deadlines and ideas. I write self-help books, I outline thrillers.

I used to write romance, but honestly, I don't think people care about love these days. Everyone's so practical.

And me? I just want my independence. I can't marry anyone. I have my own trust issues now, and I don't have the time or energy to invest in another person.

I stare at the screen for a second, then type her back, **"Why do you want to meet, Saloni?"**

Maybe it's the money. Maybe she's just another person looking for something she didn't care about when I had nothing. If that's true, then it's a sad, sad world.

My phone buzzes again.

"Rishi, I know you're still mad. And you have a reason for that. But maybe, for the last time, can we meet, please?"

Chapter-2

I'm Saloni. I'm 32 years old, and I'm back in India after 4 long years. I moved here for my job with a multinational company, but as soon as my flight landed at Mumbai airport, just one person filled my mind.

Rishi, my old lover.

I thought this chapter is closed when I was in Canada. I guess I was wrong. Why I didn't think that India will always remind me of him. And I miss him already just in three days.

I know he is a big name now. Even in Canada, everyone reads his books. But that's not why I miss him. I always believed he would make it as a writer. I loved his stories when no one else did, and I knew he had the potential all along.

But what bothers me now is he doesn't write romance novels anymore. All he writes is mostly thriller or non-fiction. I worry that he has lost his touch for romance, and that makes me sad. He has such a gift for it.

Maybe I'm the reason he lost his inspiration!

The last time we talked, he sounded low. But I was so much focused on my career in Canada, and I couldn't give him the time he needed. I wasn't ready for the heavy messages he sent me, so I ghosted him until he stopped reaching out. I'm not proud of that, but I thought it was best for both of us since we were in different countries. And later it faded away. I was too busy working, that I thought he was a distraction who affected my work.

But now, it's been three days since I returned to India, and all I do is miss him. Everywhere I go, I think of him, wishing he could just appear from somewhere... Why?

But I assume he's too busy meeting his lady fans. And I'm happy for him.

Still, I miss him. A lot. I just want to see him... one last time.

Maybe I should text him. What's the worst that could happen? He might ignore me, but I think I can handle that.

But what if he has deleted my number? Or worse, what if he forgot me?

No, he can't forget me!

Ugh, maybe it's a bad idea to text him. But I really want to see him, even if it's just for closure.

Okay, I'll text him.

Ahhh! I'm so nervous.

Fuck it. Let's see what happens!

"Hey, I'm back in India. Can we meet?" I send.

.

.

.

.

Shit! Shit!

I shouldn't have sent that.

I feel embarrassed. What will he think after all these years?

I doubt he'll reply. God, I hate myself for doing this.

And why should he reply? He's probably dating someone now.

Okay, time to sleep. "Don't worry, girl."

I shouldn't have left things this way with him.

"Why do you want to meet, Saloni?" Rishi texts.

Oh! He still remembers me. That feels good!

Well, maybe more than just good.

.

.

I write, "**Rishi, I know you're still mad. And you have a reason for that. But maybe for the last time, can we meet, please?**"

Fingers crossed!

Another message pops up in just two minutes.

"**Are you in Mumbai?**" he texts.

"**Yes,**" I answer quickly.

I hope he's in Mumbai too, but I'd travel anywhere if he wants to see me.

"**Okay. Meet me at Horizon Hotel, coffee place at 2 noon tomorrow,**" he texts.

"**Great! I will be there,**" I reply.

I sigh.

I'm so happy but at the same time feeling so nervous right now that I don't think I'll be able to sleep tonight! What should I wear tomorrow? Oh! That's a huge problem.

Don't panic! Everything will be fine.

I can't be late. I need to be early, just in case. What if he gets there first? I want to make a good impression. Should I wear something casual or dress up a bit?

I rummage through my closet, pulling out a few options. A simple white blouse? Too plain. That red dress I used to love? Maybe too much.

In the end, I settle on a fitted black top and my favorite jeans. They always made me feel confident. I'll pair them with my comfy sneakers—easy to walk in, but still cute.

Okay, this is it. I take a deep breath, trying to calm my racing heart.

I glance at the clock. It's already late, but sleep feels impossible. I just hope he still feels something for me, too. I can't help but think about all the moments we shared.

What will we talk about tomorrow?

Just be yourself, I remind myself. It's been so long, but I want him to see the real me.

I can't wait!

Chapter-3

Saloni has been waiting at the coffee place for half an hour, but she doesn't mind. She's patient, not once glancing at the big clock on the wall. A soft, content smile stays on her face, her excitement quietly bubbling underneath.

A waitress approaches her table, smiling warmly. "Ma'am, do you need anything?"

"No, I'm fine. I'm waiting for someone," Saloni replies gently.

"Okay," the waitress nods and walks away, leaving her alone with her thoughts.

A few more minutes pass, and finally, Rishi walks in. As soon as he enters, the staff immediately stand up, waving and greeting him, "Good afternoon, sir."

Rishi's eyes quickly find Saloni sitting at her table. He pauses for a moment, taking her in, before smiling and waving at her.

Saloni waves back, her heart beating a little faster. She stands as he approaches, and they share a quick, slightly awkward hug.

Sitting down, Saloni leans forward and whispers, "Thanks for coming."

There's a brief, awkward silence between them, both unsure how to navigate this moment after so long.

Saloni breaks the ice with a smile. "Everyone knows you here?"

Rishi chuckles. "Yeah, maybe because I own this hotel now... well, with three other partners."

Her eyes widen, clearly surprised. "Wow, Really?" She shakes her head, genuinely amazed. "I'm so happy for you," she says, her voice full of sincerity.

"Yeah," he says. "Anyway, how are you? And how's your work going in Canada?"

"Work is great. Actually, I've joined a company in Mumbai," she replies, her smile bright.

"Oh!" Rishi responds, shaking his head slightly, like he's trying to mask his surprise—or maybe disappointment. "So, you've moved here?"

"Yeah." She smiles again, watching his reaction. "You don't seem too happy about it, do you?"

"No, I'm fine. I'm happy. Why wouldn't I be?" he says, but the hesitation in his voice betrays him.

The tension lingers for a moment, before Rishi shifts in his seat. "Wait, I'll be right back. I'm just going to the washroom," he adds quickly, standing up and leaving the table in an awkward rush.

Saloni watches him go, her smile faltering just a little.

"I don't think he likes me anymore," Saloni thinks to herself, glancing at the big clock on the wall. It's been ten minutes, and Rishi still hasn't come back.

Feeling disappointed, she slowly stands up, ready to leave. But just as she's about to walk away, a tap on her shoulder makes her turn around. A young woman is standing there, smiling politely.

"Ma'am, please don't leave. Sir will be back in a few minutes," the girl says. "He's been... moody these days, so please don't take it personally."

Saloni, confused, asks, "And you are?"

"I'm his manager, Lily," the girl answers with a bright smile.

"Oh, okay." Saloni smiles back and gestures to the chair. "Please, sit."

As Lily sits down, Saloni takes a quick glance at her, noticing her well-put-together appearance. She can't help but say, "You're beautiful, Lily."

Lily blushes slightly at the compliment. "Thank you."

"Anyways," Saloni continues, her curiosity getting the better of her, "so, tell me... why has he been so moody these days?"

Lily lets out a small sigh. "He's been really busy lately, with work and everything. And, well, he's also about to start writing a romance fiction again after so long. It's been stressing him out a bit."

Saloni's eyes widen slightly at the mention of romance. "Is there... any girl in his life right now? I'm just asking," she says, trying to sound casual.

Lily pauses for a moment. "I don't know ma'am."

Rishi returns to the table, a small smile playing on his lips. "Ladies, I guess you two have met?"

Lily gives Saloni a polite nod before excusing herself. "Bye, Saloni," she says, walking away and leaving the two alone.

Rishi takes his seat and offers a quick apology. "I'm sorry, I had to take a call."

"It's okay, Rishi," Saloni responds, then pauses. "I know it's really awkward between us right now, but can we forget everything for a bit and just have a good talk?"

He nods. "Yes, you're right."

"Thank you." She smiles, then after a moment of hesitation, she adds, "So, I heard you're writing a romance book?"

Rishi shifts in his seat, his eyes flicking toward Lily, who's now sitting a couple of tables away, before turning his attention back to Saloni. "Yeah, you're right. It's been a long time, so I thought I should try my hand at romance again."

Saloni's face lights up with enthusiasm. "Yeah, you should! Can I know anything about the book?" she asks, curiosity gleaming in her eyes.

"It's about a girl I was dating... until last month," Rishi says, his voice casual but with a hint of something deeper. "I thought it could make a good story to tell."

Saloni's mood shifts instantly at the mention of another girl, but she manages to keep her expression neutral, not letting her disappointment show. "I'm sorry about the girl," she says, her tone light but supportive. "But I hope this will be your best work yet."

"Yeah, I hope so." Rishi sighs, his eyes briefly distant. He falls silent for a moment, as if lost in thought, before breaking the quiet with a question. "Anyways, what about you? Dating anyone?"

Saloni shakes her head. "No. I've been off the dating scene for about a year now."

Rishi's eyebrows raise slightly in surprise, but he says nothing.

Saloni continues, "I'm mostly focused on work these days. It keeps me busy." She's biting her lips hiding some emotion.

"Yeah, sometimes taking time for yourself is quite relaxing," Rishi says, his tone softening. "And, I'm happy that you're back in India."

"You are?" Saloni asks, her eyes searching his face for some deeper meaning.

"Yeah, why wouldn't I be?" he responds, offering a small smile, though there's a hint of uncertainty in his voice.

Another silence settles between them, the weight of unspoken words hanging in the air.

Rishi clears his throat and glances around. "Hey, do you remember when we used to come to this coffee place?"

Saloni blushes slightly, feeling shy. "Yeah, I do. And I also remember how we always struggled with money to afford a room in this hotel." She glances at him with a playful grin. "Wait, is that why you bought the whole hotel? Out of ego?" She gasps and laughs.

Rishi smiles, shaking his head. "No, I didn't need to prove to anyone that I'm rich. I bought this place because... I think I've always loved being here."

"Yeah, I know you loved this place," she says, her voice filled with enthusiasm, catching the nostalgia in his eyes.

He interrupts, his tone a little softer. "And I kept coming here after you left." He pauses, as if choosing his next words carefully. "I've written most of my stories in this very cafeteria."

Saloni feels her chest tighten and struggles to meet his gaze. "I'm sorry, Rishi," she whispers, her voice tinged with regret.

Rishi shakes his head gently. "No, it's okay. I'm fine now. No hard feelings." He smiles faintly. "Actually, I'm glad we discovered this place together."

A wave of emotion washes over Saloni.

I want to hug you, she thinks but doesn't say. Instead, she offers a warm smile. "I'm glad too, Rishi. And I can't tell you how proud I am of you. The person you've become... you inspire so many people, including me. It's all because you never gave up on your dreams."

Rishi smirks with a hint of bitterness in his eyes. "I didn't give up on us for a long time, either." But then he realised he shouldn't have said that. He bite his lips.

Saloni's heart sinks at his words. "Look, I'm sorry. How can I put this... I was selfish, okay? I was so focused on my work in Canada that I forgot how beautiful we were together." Her voice cracks, and she breaks down in tears.

Without hesitation, Rishi reaches over and passes her a tissue. She wipes her eyes, trying to regain her composure. "But if you want, we can make it work now," Saloni says.

Rishi sighs, like secretly he wants to hear those words, but he remains calm. He replies, "I don't know, Saloni if it's a good idea," he says, his tone measured.

She nods, accepting his uncertainty.

"But I'll think about it," he says, hoping to keep their connection alive for now.

And suddenly, a man appears out of nowhere. "Excuse me! Are you Rishi Barman?" he asks, standing just in front of them.

Rishi turns to face him and replies, "Yes."

With enthusiasm, the man continues, "Oh, sir, it's great to finally meet you! I'm a big fan of yours. Also, my wife. I loved your book *Let's Heal Together*. It's the best self-help book I've read. Thank you! And I must say, you are one bold writer."

"Thank you so much, sir," Rishi responds humbly, sensing the interruption. "But right now, I'm in the middle of something."

"Oh, I'm sorry! I won't take up too much of your time. Just an autograph, please. It would make my day!"

"Yeah, of course. Why not?" Rishi replies with a smile.

The man rushes to his table and returns with a cricket bat, grinning as he hands it to Rishi.

"What's your name?" Rishi asks as he takes the bat.

"It's Kanan… Kanan Ray," he replies eagerly.

Saloni stifles a giggle, watching Rishi write on the bat. Rishi scribbles, "All the best, Kanan, for your future. Lots of love."

"Thank you so much, sir! Have a nice day," Kanan says, beaming as he shakes Rishi's hand before leaving.

"You have a lot of fans," Saloni says with a smile. "I mean, even in Canada, I've seen people reading your books."

"Oh, I forgot to mention. Last year, I was in Canada for a week… to promote my book," Rishi replies.

Saloni's brow furrows. "Why didn't you call me then?"

Just then, his phone rings. He glances at the screen and answers, "Okay, I'll be right there."

After hanging up, he looks at her. He hurriedly says, "Sorry, I have to go. A very important meeting came up."

"Oh! That's sad. I wanted to talk to you more," she says, disappointment creeping into her voice.

"Actually, I wanted to talk too. But this is really important," he responds, his tone reluctant.

"Yeah! You should go," she replies, trying to sound supportive.

Rishi shakes his head, a hint of sadness in his expression.

He stands up and calls for Lily. She comes over, and Rishi pulls Saloni into a quick hug. "See you soon," he says, and starts to leave with Lily.

Saloni watches them go, feeling a twinge of disappointment.

But then Rishi rushes back, and Saloni's smile returns.

He faces her, his expression brightening. "I have a better idea. Why don't you stay here for tonight? I'll get you a room. If I can find the time, I'll come back, and we can continue our conversation."

She blushes, her heart racing. "Yeah… yeah. I think that's a great idea." She continues smiling with her eyes.

"Okay, now I really have to go," he says, glancing at the clock.

"All the best for your meeting," she calls, waving her hand.

He smiles back, a mix of urgency and warmth in his eyes before hurrying away.

Chapter 4

(Saloni's POV)...

I'm in room number 309 of one of the best hotels I've ever stayed in. I'm glad he offered me a room, but I can't spend the rest of the night like this... alone.

I know he's coming here tonight, and I can tell he still has feelings for me; it's in his eyes. I think that's why he bought this hotel—it holds a special meaning for us. He's always been the romantic type.

I wish I was that romantic.

Well, I have feelings for him too. And after meeting him today, I notice how he talks so mature now, and he's sincere; it turns me on a little. And how he was controlling his emotions during our conversation, that's a new Rishi. He's always been an emotional guy, a writer at heart, but now he's a professional who attends business meetings and is serious about his career. He's powerful now.

Well, *power attracts me.*

Not his money though; Anyone can earn money.

###

My phone rings. *Oh, it's him.* I can't help but blush—he's finally calling me at 11 at night. I've been waiting for him all evening but I'm not mad; I'm far-far away from being mad. I'm just happy our paths have crossed again.

I answer, my voice playful, "Hello, Mr. Writer. Why aren't you here?"

But there's no response.

Then I hear something—a sniffle. Is he crying?

"Rishi, what's wrong?" I ask, my tone shifting to worry. Silence. "Rishi?" I whisper.

His voice cracks when he finally speaks. "I can't do this again, Saloni. I want to, but I can't. I'm sorry. You have no idea what I've been through these past years. You have... no idea." He sounds angry, hurt.

I freeze, unsure of what to say. How can I tell him how sorry I am? Will he even understand? "Can you forgive me?" I ask softly, pleading. "I know it's hard. But can you? Please?"

"What would you have done in my place?" he fires back, his voice sharp.

"Well..." I begin, but he cuts me off.

"Do you know I came to see you in Canada?"

"What?" I gasp in shock.

"Last year," he continues, his voice pained, "When I went to promote my book in Canada, I contacted Atul to get your office address. I went there, sat in my car, just hoping to catch a glimpse of you. And then I saw you... walking out, holding hands with some white guy, looking so happy. It shattered me all over again. You can't imagine how many times I've been hurt because of you. I don't know if I can love again."

"Of course, you can, Rishi," I cry softly. "Just give me some time. I'll fix everything, I swear. Just like before."

"Can you, Saloni? Really?" His voice carries a painful doubt.

"Yes, I promise," I say, my voice trembling. "Trust me."

He sighs, his hesitation evident. "I don't know if I can trust you again. Not just you... I don't know if I can trust anyone anymore."

"Please, don't say that." My heart sinks at his words. "If you don't want me, I'll go. I'll leave. But don't say you can't trust anyone."

There's a long silence. Finally, he speaks, his voice heavy. "After you, I dated two girls. Both were beautiful, loyal... everything I thought I wanted. But I couldn't commit to them. I just didn't feel... attached."

My tears are falling, because I'm unable to control them.

"Is there anything I can do to help you trust again?" I ask, my voice barely above a whisper.

"I don't know." He pauses, his words heavy with thought. "But I don't think getting back together is a good idea... if that's what you're hoping for. Maybe... not right now. I just... I don't need you in my life at the moment."

I fall silent, absorbing the weight of his words. Deep down, I know he's right.

"Stay in touch, Saloni... Bye." He cuts the call.

"Bye, Rishi," I whisper, knowing this is the end of something we once had.

To be continued…

Support the Author!

REVIEW THE BOOK ON AMAZON!